HER *beastly* BLESSING

A PLAIN FAIRY TALE

ENDORSEMENTS

"Naomi Miller is a talented and wonderful author, and I can't wait to read more of her stories."

~ Molly Morris Jebber, author of
Two Suitors for Anna

About ***Ashes To Amish***

"Tucked between the covers is one powerful message about forgiveness and love."

~ *Shirley Chapel*

"What a wonderful story of love and hope! I was hooked from the first chapter. I would highly recommend this book."

~ *Toni Shiloh*, author of
Risking Love

"I was pulled in to the story line from the first pages, and didn't want to put it down after I had started it. The reader who enjoys Amish fiction will certainly enjoy this one."

~ *Ann Ellis*

"It was a pleasure to read this book. I look forward to reading other books from this author."

~ *Miss Tina's Amish Book Reviews*

"I COULDN'T PUT THIS BOOK DOWN IT WAS JUST THAT GREAT."

~ *STACEY MINTER*

"NAOMI MILLER HAS CRAFTED A WELL WRITTEN STORY WITH WONDERFUL CHARACTERS THAT CAPTURES THE FEELINGS OF THE AMISH COMMUNITY AND THE LONGING PERHAPS FOR SIMPLER TIMES. I WAS COMPLETELY DELIGHTED BY THIS STORY."

~ *AMAZON REVIEWER*

ABOUT *BLUEBERRY CUPCAKE MYSTERY*

"I MUST SAY IT WAS AMAZING! I WOULD BE PERFECTLY HAPPY TO READ MORE BOOKS BY NAOMI MILLER."

~ *VINE VOICE*

"I'M READY TO PULL UP A CHAIR IN THE SWEET SHOP, SAVOR A SLICE OF CINNAMON BREAD, AND DIG INTO THIS JUICY MYSTERY."

~ *DANA MENTINK – MULTI PUBLISHED, AWARD WINNING AUTHOR*

"I WAS PULLED INTO THE STORY FROM THE VERY FIRST SENTENCE, AND COULDN'T PUT IT DOWN UNTIL I FINISHED THE LAST SENTENCE."

~ *AMAZON REVIEWER*

HER *beastly* BLESSING

A PLAIN FAIRY TALE

NAOMI MILLER

RUTH MILLER

But the LORD said... Look not on his countenance, or on the height of his stature... for the LORD seeth not as man seeth; for man looketh on the outward appearance, but the LORD looketh on the heart.

GLOSSARY

The German/Dutch dialect spoken by the Amish is not a written language. It is solely dependent on the location and origin of each settlement. The spellings below are approximations.

ach = Oh (exclamation)
allrecht = all right
danki = thank you
Dat = Dad
Dietsch = Pennsylvania Dutch
Englisch/Englischer = non-Amish person
freind/freinden = friend/friends
Gotte = God
Gudemariye = Good morning
gut = good
in lieb = in love
jah = yes
kaffe = coffee
kapp = head covering
kumme = come
Mamm = Mom
nee = no
Ordnung = rules for Amish life
rumschpringe = running around time for youth
verhuddelt = mixed up/confused
wunderbaar = wonderful

A NOTE FROM THE AUTHORS

Hello lovely reader,

Thank you for picking up our new novel. Hope you enjoy fairy tales as much as we do.

There are many aspects of plain living that sound like a real-life fairy tale to us. If it were possible to have a bit of technology *(it's nearly impossible to write these days without a computer)* and still live plain, we would do it in a heartbeat.

A couple of notes for you: while there are many Amish communities to chose from, we chose to create our own fictional communities close to or within well-known Amish areas so that we do not accidentally imitate any actual members of the Amish community.

Also, we have taken a bit of creative license; both in the Amish communities and in the fairy tales presented in these stories. Please understand that this is done, not out of a lack of research or respect, but strictly in the interest of the story itself.

God bless!

Prologue

Everything happened so quickly.

They were traveling in a van with several other young couples from their small community, heading home from a day in the city. Everyone was quiet, thoughts floating through their heads of the wunderbaar time they had spent together.

One minute, they were moving along the dark highway at a clip that always had Dawn clinging tightly to him, something he would never have reason to complain about.

The next minute, bright lights filled the small space, there was a horrendous noise, then everything went dark.

*   *   *

When Aden woke, the first thing he noticed was the pain. He hurt everywhere—but there was also a strange numbness that kept him from getting worked up too much about it.

However, the thought of Dawn had him struggling to move his unresponsive body until he could feel gravel and dirt beneath his palms.

He tried calling out for her, but there was so much noise all around him, he could barely even hear his own voice. Somewhere nearby, he could hear someone screaming, but he couldn't identify the voice. He hoped it was not his sweet Dawn. There was no telling how badly she had been hurt.

Perhaps she was not so silly after all to protest such speeds.

The thought soured the moment it passed through his mind, leaving behind anger and regret.

Using all the strength he could muster, he found that he could do little more than push himself to his hands and knees. He took a deep breath, then began crawling, calling out for Dawn as he moved slowly across the ground.

He moved around a small hill and the screaming began to make sense. The scene before him was horrific. One vehicle lay in the middle of the road on its side, flames consuming the already blackened hulk of what had been their ride back to town.

Further ahead, quite a distance from the burning van, another vehicle lay upside down in a sea of glass and twisted metal, resting in such a way that he could see the top of what would have been the cab was clearly smashed in.

The screams he had heard earlier were coming from that direction, but he was focused on the delicate form that lay crumpled on the pavement in front of him, only a few feet from the edge of the road.

Using the small hill beside him, Aden persisted until he finally pushed his way to his feet. He stumbled as he moved forward as quickly as his feet would carry him. When he reached her, he dropped to his knees again, pulling her unresisting body into his arms.

Agony ripped through him when he looked down at her. Parts of her sweet face were covered in blood and what he hoped was dirt. Her arms as well.

Her dress was ripped. It was also covered in the same dark substances that covered her face and arms. He gently shook her, being careful not to hurt her any more than the accident had already.

He rasped out her name, shaking her gently, and then harder when there was no response.

He pulled her close, praying with everything within him that she would be *allrecht*—and that was the moment when he realized she was not breathing.

For the first time in his life, he wished he was not Amish. He wished he had one of those ridiculous phones the *Englischers* carried around everywhere with them. He would be able to call someone who could help his Dawn then for sure and for certain.

When he heard sirens in the distance, he thanked *Gotte*—then he begged *Gotte* to forgive him for not having faith; for not trusting that *Gotte* would send them help.

"They're coming, Dawn. They'll be here soon, Love. Help is on the way."

If the river had no rocks, it would not have a song.

~ Amish Proverb

One

Peter moved slowly through the nearly dark house.

"I don't know how you can work in such gloomy surroundings and yet produce such beautiful carvings." He shook his head at the sound of a grunt that was his cousin's typical response.

He moved over toward the front of the room, where there was the most light, and marveled again at the gift *Gotte* had blessed his cousin with. How those scarred hands could form such beauty from rough wood, Peter would never truly understand. He was hopeless when it came to carving anything.

But bring beauty from ugliness Aden could most decidedly do, for sure and for certain. The shops in town sold his pieces faster than he could possibly carve them.

The *Englischer* tourists who came into town sure enough went on and on about how difficult it was to believe that human hands were responsible for such intricate detail.

Many of them wished to meet the artist, but Aden had refused to set one foot anywhere near town since leaving the hospital and returning home nearly three years ago, except for one, brief visit.

At first it had been necessary. His injuries were severe. The doctors had told him to avoid people as much as possible. With his body weakened, he could not afford to contract some illness and set his recovery back.

Then there had been his first—and final—visit to town before ending up in the hospital again. The details of that visit Aden had never shared with Peter, but from his cousin's reaction whenever Peter mentioned going into town, he was fairly certain it would just be better not to ever ask.

Since Aden's return, and almost immediate self-imposed exile, Peter had been sent to care for his cousin, running errands for him, helping him around the house, driving him anywhere he wished to go, if he wished to go anywhere, which he had not.

So, instead of asking his cousin if he wanted to go to town, Peter continued to run errands for him. He cheerfully did all of Aden's shopping and took care of any deliveries. He made certain to deliver his cousin's work to be sold promptly, and returned with whatever the people in the community sent to him.

Peter's mother, especially, was always one to send food, bread, pies and other treats to Aden. She had written up several lists for Peter each week when he headed out to get Aden's groceries, determined that her nephew must not be eating right.

She had even tried sending over treats with several of the young women in the community, all with near disastrous results. Aden had not exactly slammed the door in their faces, but it had been nearly so and now none of the young women involved would even consider going to his home again.

Peter had been in the house for one of the visits, after which he had told his *mamm* that she was wasting her time. He knew that Aden needed to heal—and in more ways than one. His spirit and his heart needed just as much time, if not more, than his body.

He had made that point to her, and then

to several of her *freinden* as well, when they had sent their *dochders* over to deliver things to Aden. He'd been able to intercept several of them, saving the treats they had brought, and soothing their ruffled feathers, as well.

However, the unexpected visits always put Aden in a terrible mood. That was when he had begun to lower the lights inside and covered the windows of his home, first the ones that faced the front, and then the rest.

Even after his body had healed and his scars had begun to fade, Aden had refused to leave home for anything but Sunday services.

More than a little concerned over his isolation, and unwilling to leave his cousin alone too much, Peter had continued to care for him. He was determined that he would drop by every day and, thankfully, Aden did not argue with him.

At each and every visit he tried to uncover just one window. There were times when Aden left it alone until after Peter left, but most days he would walk right over to it and close the thick curtains tightly with a growl or a grunt, and then turn and go back to work.

The lights were another matter entirely. No plain home had all that many mirrors inside. As a general rule, they were a people who rejected vanity, but Peter had made a point to remove every reflective surface and mirror, other than the one in Aden's bathroom, before he had *kumme* home from the hospital.

It had made no difference. Aden had turned the lights lower and lower every week, somehow learning to adjust to the near absence of light.

And somehow he had learned not only to live, but to work with the light so low, it was sometimes a struggle for Peter to even see to move around. But Aden's work had not suffered. In fact, and Peter was loathe to actually say it where his cousin could hear, but many people said Aden's carvings were even better since the accident.

When he had first begun hearing the comment, Peter had wanted to reprimand them, to tell them not to say such a hurtful thing. Then, once he had realized they were not being unkind, he had thought it must be that they were being charitable.

But eventually he had been forced to admit, after comparing Aden's older and newer works, that his cousin's work was indeed much improved since the accident.

Aden certainly treated his carving differently since the accident. It was no longer just something he did in his spare time... or something he did to save up for marriage. It was his only purpose in life, it seemed.

Peter had asked his cousin about it, concerned at first that he might be pushing himself to carve because he felt he must. Aden had mostly ignored him.

After returning from the hospital,

several weeks had past before Aden had picked up a tool. Then, even after he had, there had been many more days where he only stood, staring at his blocks of wood.

Then, without any warning, one day Peter had arrived to find Aden hard at work on a piece. He had lost much of the speed he'd had before the accident, but none of the skill. Even his badly damaged muscles remembered what to do with the tools.

Aden had carved for hours that day, more than making up for whatever he might have lost in speed. After that, carving had become a daily exercise for him, until he had regained all of his lost speed and accuracy—and a skill that was something akin to amazing.

Aden had remarked more than once to his cousin that his carving was a saving grace. And even though Peter had initially worried, he felt certain he knew what his cousin meant. If he'd been stuck inside with absolutely nothing to do, he might have gone crazy.

Of course, even though Aden kept busy and always insisted that he was just fine, Peter and his *mamm* worried that he had not mourned as he should. He certainly had not moved on, as the community had expected him to do.

He'd barely left his little house, much less ventured out into the world again, in the last three years. He attended Sunday service, but always sat in the very back and left quickly, not participating in fellowship or any of the singings the youth held.

He just sat there in his little house every day, carving one piece of wood, then another... one project after another.

Dawn's family had grieved and then had moved on. As had the families of the others who had been killed in the crash. As the only survivor, Aden had no one else to talk with about how it felt to be alive, how the crash had affected them, how living without the others in the crash had changed them.

He was alone in that, just as he was alone in his house, and with his injuries.

Peter had no clue how to snap his cousin out of his self-imposed isolation, though he prayed for his cousin every day, as many of their friends did. They all worried about him in their own ways, but no one had any idea about how to bring Aden to his senses.

The youth had tried. They had even visited Aden. He tolerated them when he felt like it, but not often... and mostly just the boys.

The bishop was the only person aside from Peter that Aden never turned away. The bishop had been friends with Aden since before the accident.

Peter never asked, but he figured that Aden must have carved something special for the bishop, his wife, or one of their families before the accident, and they had ended up being *gut* friends because of it.

He visited Aden at least once a week. Peter always made himself scarce when the bishop arrived, feeling that he would be intruding on something personal or private. Aden had never suggested he stay, and neither had the bishop.

Two

Beth pedaled her ancient bicycle down the narrow lane, careful to stay within the well-worn rut beside the pavement that had clearly been carved by the passage of countless bicycles and scooters over the years.

The dark clouds in the sky above her had promised rain for some time now, but she'd been hopeful she could make it home before they emptied their stored up precipitation onto her head.

As she pedaled, she thought about her class... about the book she had started reading the evening before... and about this new, little community they had moved to recently.

Everyone so far had been nice, but—as was typical with a small, close-knit community—they had also kept their distance. It was something she was accustomed to, having moved many times since her *mamm's* passing.

She and *Dat* had tried to find a place where they could feel at home many times, with no success so far. He built clocks and she taught the scholars, so their new homes often came from finding an advertisement in the Budget from a town in need of a new teacher.

Each town started out feeling as if it might be the right place. Beth and her *dat* would find a house, move in, attend Sunday services, begin to get to know their neighbors, then she would get acquainted with the parents of her scholars, and they would try to fit themselves into the community.

But so far, not one of the towns had turned out to be a place they wanted to stay. None of them felt right.

Everyone agreed they wanted a reasonably intelligent young woman to teach the scholars, but no one ever seemed to understand her never-ending desire to read.

She would ride around town with her bag, which always contained at least one book, and sometimes two or more. She would often park her bicycle and sit under a tree or on a bench in the park, reading for an hour or more as the people walked by.

Some would nod their heads appreciatively, glad to see they had chosen their teacher well. Others would shake their heads at her wasting time with a book when there was so much else to be done.

And then, well, there were the ladies. Every town they moved to, there was a group of ladies who were determined to marry her off to someone. She had been invited to more homes to meet a young man than for any other reason she could think of.

They were always so determined in their mission. But then, so was she. After watching her parents' love, and how her *dat* mourned for her *mamm,* she knew she wanted precisely what they had found together.

That particular goal typically made her less than popular with many of the mothers and grandmothers in the community. And since it was the mothers who had children in school, it also tended to affect her teaching, after a time.

Over the years, she had grown accustomed to it. *Dat* had not. He always said that the ladies were perhaps being a bit too pushy. But then, he always made the point that he wanted her to be as happy as he had been with her mother.

If only he could see that that was precisely what she was waiting for...

* * *

When the rain started, it was just a few random, fat drops falling, but after only a few minutes the speed and concentration picked up, until the rain formed a blurry sheet of water in front of her face, and all around her,

After a few minutes, the rut she was on turned to mud. Less than a minute later the tire she'd been babying for weeks hit something and sent the bicycle skidding.

Miraculously, she came to rest just a few feet from where she'd started, in a thick patch of tall grass. It cushioned her fall considerably and she lay there for nearly a minute, catching her breath and moving her body slowly to test for injuries that would bring her right back down if she tried to stand.

Once she was fairly certain she had no serious injuries, she resolved to turn over. From there, getting to her feet was more or less an easy task, but she was getting more soaked by the second.

She had a moment to think that finding her bicycle might just be impossible, especially in the driving rain, before she spotted it lying about a foot from where she had landed.

Once she had retrieved her bicycle, she started to look for some place where she could wait out the storm. The bicycle was clearly not going to carry her home and walking two more miles in the rain would not only be nearly impossible, it would likely leave her nursing a cold.

Looking around her, it was easy to see

there was only one house nearby and no cars in sight. For the first mile, cars had passed her every few minutes, but she hadn't seen any for at least the last half of a mile.

Not so surprising with this storm.

It wasn't difficult to guess that most people were probably waiting it out wherever they were.

* * *

Aden huffed when the knocking shattered his concentration. His cousin had already been here for his daily visit and the rest of the community had long since learned to respect his self-imposed isolation. Aside from that, he had to wonder who would be out visiting in this storm.

When the knock sounded again, he set down his tools with a growl and moved toward the door, throwing it open with another huff of breath.

The sight that greeted him stole the angry words he had been prepared to hurl at the poor, apparently oblivious soul who had happened upon his doorstep.

A flash of well-timed lightning outlined the young woman standing there, who was soaked through and covered in mud. There was also no disguising the beauty that lay beneath water, mud, and clothing that looked to be ruined.

Aden inhaled sharply just as the bright light that had lit up the sky only a moment before faded to darkness again. She looked up at him then, and he was grateful for the thick rain and clouds that obscured any light in the early evening sky.

He wanted to turn her away, certain that such a lovely, delicate young woman would be repulsed and horrified by his appearance, but he knew it would be wrong to leave her out in this weather, especially since she was already soaked.

He did not recognize her. She was

certainly not one of the young women his neighbors and relatives had been sending around with treats and invitations to the youth singings. He could not remember having seen her at a Sunday service, either.

Perhaps she is visiting family in the area.

Although he knew that was not very likely. If she was visiting, she would likely not be out alone in such weather.

Before he could ask her anything, she stepped forward a little and spoke. "Oh, *gut*. You are home. I wasn't sure." Her voice was as beautiful as her face, and he was completely charmed by her obvious innocence.

So much so, he nearly stepped forward... before he remembered his own appearance. He remained where he was, blocking the doorway, but still enough in the darkened room that she should not be able to see him clearly.

They stood just like that for several

tense seconds before she spoke up again.

"Could I *kumme* in, dry off a bit?" A moment later, she added, "at least until the storm passes?" She shifted her weight from one foot to the other and quietly cleared her throat.

He wanted to say no. He wanted to step back and close the door on her, to shut her out with the rest of the world, but there was something about her that tugged at him. He couldn't bear to just shut her out.

Against his better judgement, he stepped back, and gestured with a grunt for her to come inside. Then he made his way over to the large fireplace he hadn't used in weeks, grateful for once for his cousin, who had cleaned out the hearth not long ago and laid paper, kindling and a few small logs for a new fire.

It took several minutes to get the fire going, but once it did he moved quickly away from the corner of the room before any light from the flames could illuminate his features.

"Ach. Danki." She stepped even closer to the hearth, rubbing her hands over her arms as she shivered. "For sure and for certain, I do appreciate your kindness."

"It's no problem, really." He muttered the words, still moving away as he spoke.

When she said nothing else, he moved into the kitchen, closing the door firmly behind him before turning the small gas lamp up a bit.

In the muted light, he went about heating water for tea, and gathering some of the food his cousin had brought him this afternoon. Once again, he was thankful that his aunt worried so about his eating habits. She had a habit of sending a week's worth of food along with his cousin every few days.

Most of the time, he sent half of it back with his cousin. Peter, in turn, would drop off quite a bit of it at the shelter in town where he volunteered several days a week.

Aden was certain the people who received those deliveries were more than grateful... and likely more deserving than he.

When the water had boiled, and he had set out cups and plates on a small tray, he turned and reached for the gas lamp, turning the light down just as the kitchen door opened, and the young woman before him let out a small squeak.

"*Ach.* You frightened me." Her words came out with her breath, sounding much like air escaping from a balloon.

The muscles in his gut tightened in response, sending a deep, restless churning throughout him. He wondered at it, and then, when he recognized a reaction that he had not felt since before Dawn's death, he clenched his teeth and forced his mind elsewhere.

He did not want to think about what those feelings meant. Not now. Not with her. He wasn't ready. He didn't want to be ready. The memory of losing Dawn was still much too fresh, much too painful.

To her, he merely grunted, more than a little annoyed at his reaction to her closeness. Why would she come into his kitchen uninvited? Was it not enough that she had invaded his home... his sanctuary... his solitude?

How did she have to be right there in his way, with her appealing face and delicate build, and the air of vulnerability that simply hung around her?

Three

Thankful that he had already turned down the light in the kitchen, Aden waited for his guest to take the hint and back up.

It took nearly a minute for her to realize that he was waiting for her to move. And when she did, her movements were almost ridiculously slow. She backed up slowly, putting out a hand to feel for the door frame she had just walked through in the sudden darkness. Then she finally turned and moved through the doorway.

He followed a few moments later, forcing himself to take deep breaths to calm himself. Aside from the anger that filled him, there were other emotions invading his mind and body that he did not care to examine at the moment.

He wanted her dry and out of his house the moment the storm let up. He would drive her home himself if need be, but he wanted her gone, away, out of his home—and his life.

The last thing he needed was some helpless woman interfering in his life, asking him questions he had no answers for, expecting explanation he didn't care to give, taking up time—time that he had so carefully filled with his work.

It didn't really matter that he had time to spare, that he did almost nothing but carve most days... or read. He had no desire to share any of his time with another person right now. It was difficult enough dealing with his nosy cousin most days.

The only reason he tolerated those visits was because the young man came in handy for running errands and making deliveries. If not for his help, Aden would have had to find some way to do those things himself—and that would mean letting more people see him. And he was simply not ready for that.

He followed the young woman, who had moved back to where she had been standing in front of the fire before he'd retreated to the kitchen. He set the tray down on the little table beside her, but said nothing. She would figure out what to do with the tray, he was sure.

He was right. She turned and started to make her tea and place some of the wonderful banana bread his aunt had sent over onto a small plate.

While she helped herself, he went back

to his carving. He carved silently while she ate and sipped tea in front of the fire, and the rain pounded overhead.

They stayed just like that for a long time, her sipping her tea, and him carving on a chunk of wood.

By the time the sound of rain on the roof had begun to slow, he had nearly forgotten she was there... nearly. Of course, her voice reminded him quickly enough.

"Thank you for your hospitality, but I should probably head home now." Her voice was exceptionally quiet, and soft. It was such a gentle reminder that a woman was in his house, in his space.

He was not quite ready to stop working, so he remained where he sat... until she headed for the front door. It was then he remembered catching a glimpse of her bicycle when she had stepped into the house. The state it had been in, she would certainly not be riding it home, and he was not about to force her to walk.

"Wait. I'll take you. You're not going to be able to ride your bike and I don't think it will be all that easy to push, either."

"Really, you don't have to." She spoke softly, but he could hear that relief in her voice.

"Nonsense. It's no trouble." He insisted. And finally, he put his chisel down.

* * *

When Aden lifted the broken bicycle into the back of the buggy his cousin used to haul the wood he used to carve, and the finished pieces, the rain had all but stopped.

However, the sky above them was still not clear, which he was somewhat grateful for. The clouds would help to hide his face and hands, but at least the rain had completely stopped.

He walked around to help the still shivering young woman into the seat. Then, as he walked around the buggy, he tucked the thick scarf a bit tighter about his neck, then he climbed up and took hold of the reins.

He reached into the back seat of the buggy and flipped a thick blanket out over her lap. She sighed and snuggled into it, pulling it up over her arms as she settled onto the seat beside him.

He navigated the bumpy, rut filled driveway his cousin had been at him to repair for almost a year. It hadn't exactly been in wonderful condition when he had bought the house, but at the time he'd told himself he would eventually get to it.

There were many things he had meant to get done over the years, but since it no longer mattered what his house looked like, with no wife and no family and almost no visitors, he worried less and less about things that needed doing and concentrated on his carving—his one escape, his one distraction, his one saving grace.

Thinking of it now though, he had to admit that it would be a lot nicer, even for him, if the driveway were in a bit better repair.

Just like so many other things around here.

Looking back at the house as they pulled out onto the road, he could see several things that were in need of obvious repair. Why had he let so many things go for so long?

It was true, he had no wife to bring here, but he did have a few visitors. They would likely enjoy visiting more if they were coming to a nice house, not one that looked as if it was in desperate need of repair.

For sure and for certain any Englischers who drive by must have some odd ideas about the house as well.

He knew enough about *Englischers* to know that they would likely *kumme* up with some silly story about ghosts or spirits when they spoke of his house.

He knew there were enough of them who drove by it each day. They would certainly have seen how it looked, tall grass growing up in many places around the house—a house that was in desperate need of paint and shutters and a bit of care.

Once he had decided something needed to be done about all of the repairs he had let go for too long, Aden realized how much better he felt about the whole situation.

He would get to work on it right away.

* * *

The young woman on the seat next to him chattered almost the whole way through town, asking him questions at first, to which he only replied in grunts or one word answers. Once she figured out she was not going to draw him into conversation, she still talked, but she stopped waiting for him to say anything in response.

She went on about things he only half listened to, until she mentioned a book she was reading. That caught his attention, though he still said nothing.

But he did listen more intently after that. He was surprised to discover that she was very well read. And, not only had she read quite a few of the same books he had read, she sounded as though she had enjoyed them as much as he had. Even Dawn had not enjoyed all of the books he had tried to share with her.

Clearly the young woman he was driving home had read and enjoyed many of the books he had read—and owned. He wondered at her reasons. She was young, attractive, intelligent. Why would she not have some young man in the community waiting for her hand?

Part of him wanted to ask, but that same part of him knew that there was a gut chance that asking the question would give her the wrong idea about his intentions.

That was the last thing he needed, some doe-eyed young woman who thought him a handy marrying sort who was interested in her.

Yet, the more she talked about the books she loved, and why, the more curious he became. Her voice charmed him. Her intelligence intrigued him. Her obvious excitement fascinated him. She spoke knowledgeably and he was enjoying listening to her, more than he would have expected.

And then, before he could even ask, she answered one of his questions.

"Books are one of the reasons I enjoy teaching. Planting seeds in young mind, watching them grow. It is amazing, jah?"

So, she's a teacher... That would certainly explain her love of books.

He realized then that he could imagine her there quite easily, behind a desk, reading. He could see her standing in front of the classroom, writing on the blackboard, explaining things to the scholars.

The image of her sitting there reading, and the pictures in his mind of her teaching were much more appealing than he had expected them to be.

After losing Dawn, and with what had happened to him in the accident, he had never thought to actually find another woman who appealed to him again.

And he had certainly never thought he would find himself wondering and worrying over whether or not a woman could find him appealing.

Fortunately, she was perfectly content to go on about the children she taught without any contribution from him. It was a gut thing, since he was becoming more uncomfortable by the moment at just the thought of her standing up in front of her class.

He forced his attention back to the

horses, trying to get the image of her out of his mind, certain she could never see him as anything other than he was, scarred and broken. Why would someone as beautiful and sweet as she see him any other way? No, it would be best to take her home and then leave her be.

That was what he told himself the rest of the drive, all through town, and then back out into the country, up her lane, and again while he unloaded her bicycle. Even when he watched her walk up the stairs and into the little house.

It was always best not to dwell on what could never be.

And it could never be.

Four

Aden hammered the chisel into the wood, gouging out whole chunks in his anger and frustration. Wood flew in every direction as he chipped away at the massive block he had been using for just this purpose for nearly three years.

The block had been a gift from the bishop... of all people. It was an enormous piece of hardwood that was filled with knots and irregular grain. He had tried carving it at first, but after wasting more time on it than he liked to admit, he discovered that it would serve a much more satisfying purpose as something to pour his anger into.

There was absolutely nothing at all beautiful about the wood. When the bishop had brought it to him, he had said there was something about the wood that he felt strongly about, and that he was certain no one other than Aden could find beauty in it.

He had tried, for weeks, but no matter how hard he chipped away at it, there was no beauty to be found, only more of the same ugly knots and rough grain.

Then... he had found himself taking out his frustrations on the huge piece of wood one day and had decided it was much better suited to be a target for his anger and the destructive tendencies that surfaced when he thought about the accident or the loss of

Dawn.

This time, however, gouging the wood was not helping to work off his anger. With every stroke, he felt almost as if he were attacking himself, somehow making himself even more disfigured and ugly.

The strong attraction he felt for Beth haunted him. He felt as if he were being disrespectful to Dawn's memory. She had died in the accident, and he had always felt like a part of him had died with her.

For three years, he had not looked at another woman in the community, and not just because he tended to hide himself at the back of the church services, sitting as much in the darkness as possible, and not making eye contact with anyone but the preacher.

He had not raised his voice in song or attended a single gathering for the youth. He had kept to himself as much as possible, devoting his time to only his carving.

The *Englischer* store owner in town

certainly sold the pieces he carved quickly enough. The knowledge should have made him happy, but it only served to remind him that his deal with the store owner had been his way of saving money to marry Dawn in the fall... three years ago.

Now the money sat in the bank account he had opened at the local bank in town, with his name, and Dawn's name together. They had been saving for their future together.

After the accident, he had been in the hospital for some time. He had even missed the funeral for Dawn because the doctors had been far more concerned that his burns would be a danger to him out in the open, surrounded by people, susceptible to the sort of infection that could set his healing back for months.

His first trip back into the world had been to that bank, first to remove Dawn's name, and then to remove the money she had deposited so he could give it to her family.

They had tried to insist he should keep it, but he'd won that argument. The thought of keeping money she had been saving for her marriage was far too painful for him. That he had added to it was no one's business but his own.

Fortunately, his own hospital bills had wiped out most of the remainder. It had been easier for him to keep the account, with only the money he had started it with.

The money had slowly built back up over the last three years. He had used some of it each month to buy wood, tools and supplies for his work. More of it had gone to pay for food and his continuing hospital care. But, even with all of that, there was a considerable sum sitting in the bank, waiting to be used on something he could not bring himself to consider.

He had what he needed and he had no plans to spend any of the money on marriage or anything else at the moment.

The chisel stuck in the wood with what turned out to be a half-hearted attempt, and he stopped to pry it out of the half-formed gouge. He was surprised to realize that his anger was spent. With a sigh, he went to clean his tools.

Once everything was put away, he made his way through the house to the kitchen. He hadn't realized until now that he was hungry, but he was, and he needed to do something about it.

When he walked into the room, he reached for the gas lamp beside the door, turning it up a bit as he moved past it. As he did, the light fell across the discarded tray from the night before and the memory of her was like a punch in the gut.

Even from across the room, the scent of her had teased him, the fresh smell of rain and something else, something so subtle that he couldn't possibly identify it, but it haunted him along with the clenching of his gut that he knew to be desire.

The knock at the front door saved him from being forced to deal with the tray or the leftovers on it. His cousin would probably take care of the tray and the evidence of Beth's time there.

If only he could get her out of his head so easily.

*　*　*

Beth stood on the wide porch, a carefully covered pie resting in her hands while she waited for the man who had never given her his name last night to answer the door.

He had been grouchy, but he'd let her in out of the rain and he really hadn't had to. She was grateful—so grateful—for his hospitality. He had started a fire, heated water for tea, and then taken her and her broken bicycle home in his buggy.

He could have let me walk. But he didn't.

Riding the bicycle had not been an

option, and she had been thankful he had never actually expected her to try to walk home pushing the thing.

She had arrived home with her bicycle, mostly dry and with her stomach full. It was a lot to be thankful for.

Which is why you brought him the pie, silly.

She told herself it was not right to want to see him again. But when she'd gotten up that morning, and the sun was shining, she had not been able to resist making him a pie.

Since it was a Saturday, she didn't even have to wait for school to end. She had left the house as soon as the pie was cool enough to tuck it into the travel basket she'd placed in their smaller buggy.

Her *dat* had taken one look at her bicycle and just shook his head. He was accustomed to her running off the road or into small things that were difficult to notice when the rider is daydreaming, but never something quite so bad as it was now.

He'd told her he would get to work fixing it, but since it would obviously take several days for him to determine what parts he needed, she had saddled up her favorite of their three horses and attached the small buggy.

Now she was waiting for the man to open the door, hoping she didn't look as foolish as she felt, standing here on his porch with a pie. She was certain of one thing. He would most definitely be the kind of person who would tell her just how silly she looked.

When the door opened, she gasped, first because he opened the door with a jerk, then because he practically snarled at her.

"What! Did you forget how the door works?"

At her gasp, he looked down at her, as if he were noticing her for the first time. He immediately moved backward and started to shut the door.

She caught sight of his face, though it was still very much in shadow. And she knew something about it was odd, but she couldn't quite figure out what.

"Wait." She put one hand on the door, her other one holding onto the pie. "I brought this for you. It's the least I could do. You were so kind." She kept talking, hoping he would stop pushing on the door so she could hand him the pie.

She also hoped he would step into the light. She had not yet gotten a good look at his face, and it felt as if he was doing it on purpose.

They stood there, locked in a stalemate of sorts for more than a minute, while she tried to get a better look at him and he tried to push the door closed on her, until finally she decided to just set the pie down and leave it.

"Well anyway, thank you, again. I'll leave you alone now, since that's obviously what you want. Enjoy the pie."

Fortunately, he did not shut the door on her pie. He let go enough that she was able to set it down without it being smooshed. She set it down and turned from the door, moving quickly down the front steps and then toward her buggy.

When she had settled herself in the seat, she glanced quickly over toward his door. He still had not shut it, but he had backed up even further into the shadows, obviously waiting for her to leave before bending down to pick up the pie.

What is with him, I wonder?

She told herself there was absolutely no excuse for such behavior. No matter the reason he thought he might have, there was not a good enough reason to warrant rudeness.

At that point, she was almost sad she had left one of her favorite baking dishes with him. Would he return it? Would he appreciate the pie? Had she just wasted her morning, making and then delivering it to him?

"Nee." It was never a waste of time when one did something nice for someone else. She had not baked him the pie simply so that he could appreciate her. She had done it as a thank you, because she appreciated what he had done for her.

Now she could only hope that he would enjoy the pie—or else perhaps he would share the pie with someone who would enjoy it.

As she drove along the road, she marveled at how everything around her had a clean, fresh look to it this morning. There were a few tree limbs that had fallen during the storm, but mostly everything just looked as though it had benefitted from the rain.

She took her time traveling toward town, thinking about the man she had baked a pie. He was a mystery to be sure. Nothing about him would be easy to figure out, of that she was certain. But there was something about him that intrigued her.

He stayed in the shadows, as though he was afraid to let anyone see his face. He kept his house dark, but he didn't hesitate to light a fire for a cold and wet stranger who happened upon him during a storm.

He seemed to communicate mostly in grunts or body language, but the few looks she had gotten at what he was working on off to one side of his living room had told her he had truly been blessed with a talent.

Gotte had chosen to bless this man with a gift for carving, yet for some reason he was more or less hiding out in his own house.

She had to wonder why.

Perhaps there is someone in town who knows.

The idea intrigued her, but almost as soon as it came to her, she dismissed it. The people in town looked at her as though there were something wrong with her.

No one seemed to understand why she loved books so much, why education was so important to her, why she walked around with a book in front of her nose, why she didn't worry about having her head in the clouds.

She and her *dat* had moved to the sleepy little town for a fresh start. They had lived in several different towns, all with nearly the same troubling results.

As long as she was teaching, no one paid her much mind. But the moment she started to walk around town with a book in her hand, they started to whisper and stare. Their plain neighbors were not so obvious about it as the *Englischers,* but they still looked at her as if they had no idea what to do with her.

Still... since she was out and about, and she had to drive through town anyway, she decided to stop and pick up a few things at the market.

Five

When Beth turned into the tiny driveway to her house, she was still shaking her head. It had taken almost no prompting to get the people in town to talk about Aden, the young woodcarver who lived out his days now as a recluse just outside of town.

Evidently, he had been badly scarred in

an accident that had claimed the lives of his fiance and several other people from the community, including the drivers of both vehicles.

Nearly everyone in town had something to say about the accident, about the recklessness of young people driving fast cars, about the depth of loss the entire town felt after that night, about how difficult it had been for everyone involved.

They had spoken about how difficult the ordeal had been on Aden's family, but they really didn't seem to know just how the man himself had been affected by the accident... or the scars... or the loss of his fiance.

Evidently, even now, his cousin did most everything for him; ran his errands, dropped off his carvings, took him food that people in the community made up for him, what with him being a bachelor and all alone otherwise.

Everyone had specifically made the

point several times that Aden was a bachelor and—aside from his scars—was a fine young man and a *wunderbaar* part of the community. They weren't pushy about it, just more than a little obvious.

Also, pretty much everyone had agreed that his skill at carving had actually improved after the accident—the fact that he sold a great many more carvings seemed to back up their belief. Beth wondered if their opinions were based on actual improvement or if it was more to do with his carving many more items since his accident.

It made sense that he would want to keep busy since the accident. After all, he was alone most of the time.

At least she understood now why he kept his house so dark, and also why he stayed in the shadows. He was likely bothered by his scars. She could not begin to imagine how difficult it must be to carry around such constant reminders of so painful a tragedy.

And he had lost his fiance as well. There was no pain she could think of that would compare to such a loss as losing the one person you planned to spend the rest of your life with. The mere thought was heart-rending.

There was one interesting notion though. At least part of the time, she had felt as if the people in town were trying to talk Aden up.

As if he would even be interested in someone like me...

The thought made her laugh, but it also made her wonder. Were they trying to talk him up because he was a bachelor—and the community liked to marry off their bachelors—or could it have been that they were trying to match her up with someone?

In every community she had been a part of, it seemed to be their mission to match up all of the young people. Even one couple left unmatched had everyone all aflutter to *fix things.*

As she unhooked the small buggy, walked the horse into their barn, and took care of his needs and getting him settled with a little food, she thought about how life for Aden Bontrager was.

He sat there in his house day after day, obviously dealing with a tremendous amount of loss and possibly some guilt. He carved for hours on end. He must tend to his animals, but he had no farm to take care of, only his carvings.

What did he do with his spare time? She'd seen no evidence that he did much work around his house. Did he only carve huge chunks of wood? Was there anything else that brought him joy?

Not one person in town had known a thing about his hobbies, his likes or dislikes, what he did aside from carving and wallowing in his loss.

It made her wonder if he enjoyed reading. It would make sense if he did.

Sitting there alone all of the time, he really couldn't just carve every spare minute of the day. Could he?

That was when she resolved to take him a book or two. For sure and for certain he had time to read. Shouldn't he have some books available if he chose to do so?

She thought he should. And with that in mind, she decided to go inside and find him some good books, hopeful that he would accept her gesture for what it was... and that he would take great care with her precious books. She had so few, but each one was a treasure to her.

The stories within had taken her to all sorts of interesting destinations, introduced her to worlds she could never have seen in the tiny towns her father kept moving them to, and given her an appreciation for the world around them that could not be matched by anything other than her love of the written word.

Most plain communities did not put

much emphasis on reading, not one bit. She was glad that this one seemed to, at least somewhat.

She might get odd looks from the people in town, plain and not, but no one gave her a difficult time over reading, just because of how she read, and how often. One thing she noticed wherever she had lived; apparently, it was odd to read while one walked. After awhile, she decided it was best to give that activity up.

She shook her head at the idea that formed in her mind. She was accustomed to being an oddity no matter where they moved. But now, well it was an odd thing to realize that there was someone in this community who was more of a curiosity than she was.

That alone made Aden Bontrager the most interesting person she had met in this sleepy little town, and it made her want to stay and find a way to get to know him when she took him the books to read.

He might be a bit of a recluse, but there were so many things about his story that she found fascinating. And she wanted to get another look at the things in his living room that he had been carving.

Looking at the few things of his that were in the store in town—the place where she had gotten most of her information about him—had been fascinating. He was truly gifted, and she wanted to see more.

He'd been working on one piece while she was there and there had been several others scattered across the room in different degrees of completion.

Suddenly, she was curious, so much so that she nearly turned toward the barn again to saddle the horse so she could go back to his house, just to see if she could get him to let her in.

She wandered through the barn to her *dat's* workshop. He sat right where she had expected to find him, on a small bench beside the pieces of her broken bicycle.

He had an array of tools laid out, both on the bench around him and on the floor at his feet. She watched him for a long time, marveling in how much she enjoyed watching him as he worked. He sat there, completely unaware as far as she could tell, that she was standing in the doorway.

She watched him work, and thought about Aden. Would he let her watch him this way or would he shut her out?

Would he even let her in the door if she went by his house again? He hadn't let her in today and she'd been bringing him a pie. Why did she think he would let her in if she went there again? She didn't think he would, but something within her told her to try again—that it was worth taking a chance on.

She stood there in the doorway for several more minutes before pushing away and heading out of the barn and then toward the house.

Once inside, she went to the small

bedroom at the back of the house she had turned into a library of sorts. Inside that room were shelves she'd hung and bookcases she'd filled. Her *dat* had recovered a chair that was comfortable enough that she could sit and read for hours in her little personal library.

Walking over to the shelves, she read over the titles of books she had already read, thinking about the stories within the pages of each book. She knew each one so well, they felt like old, dear friends—every single one.

She had visited every place in every book, many of them time and time again. There were so many wonderful stories, she was having some difficulty figuring out which ones she should bring him.

She thought about the other night, when he had been driving her home. She had chattered on about favorite books almost the entire way to her house, but he hadn't said a word.

Perhaps it was possible he didn't enjoy reading. Was she wasting her time bringing him books? She hadn't seen any laying around his house. But then, she hadn't seen much of the house—just the living room and a bit of his kitchen.

It was possible he enjoyed reading, but wasn't much of a talker. His behavior the remainder of that evening would certainly prove that theory. He hadn't said more than a dozen words the entire evening that she could remember.

But that voice inside told her that it would be worth the try, so she pulled several of her favorites off the shelves and put them on the small table that sat beside the door, where she would be sure to pick them up on her way out.

Once she had set the books down, she settled herself in her reading chair, tucking her legs up underneath her and opening the book she had been reading most recently.

* * *

Aden looked at the pie that was now sitting on his kitchen counter in its cheery yellow dish. The scent of it was enough to have his mouth watering and he could see that she had spent a great deal of time on it. Every bit of the crust looked perfectly shaped and baked.

He knew... if the pie underneath that perfect crust tasted as *gut* as it smelled, he would be hard pressed to ignore it, so he had not cut into it yet. He hoped that, as long as it remained uncut, he could resist temptation.

The young woman who had dropped it off was another temptation he was trying to avoid. He had already discovered, completely by accident, that she was nothing like the other young women in town, which had been the first thing that had attracted him to Dawn. She too had been different from all the other young women in town, but in a very different way from Beth.

It was tripping him up, this thinking of the two of them in comparable terms. They were really nothing alike. However, they were also very much alike, in all the ways that mattered to him.

Part of him was curious about her, wondered if it would be such a bad idea to get to know her a little. Another part of him, the part that still held on so tightly to his memories of Dawn, told him it would be a bad idea.

Something about her persistence told him the choice might not be left entirely up to him anyway. She had come by, brought him a pie, left it with him... even when he had tried not to take it.

Her family had not been here long and he really knew nothing about them, but after spending the evening with her—and then watching her with the pie this morning, he could see she was not the type to give up easily.

Somehow, he knew she would be back. And something told him she would make a nuisance of herself. He wasn't sure what to think of that, either.

I wonder what she will think of my scars?

The question had no answer. Too many times in the past he had thought he knew how someone would respond to them and too many times he had been wrong. After this happened again and again, he had stopped trying to figure out anyone's reaction.

For some time now, he had simply kept out of the public eye, hiding himself away from everyone who might be bothered by his appearance, slipping away quickly after the services on Sunday and avoiding any gatherings in the community.

If he was not there for everyone to see, his appearance could not bother anyone. At least that was what he told himself. Mostly what people wanted from him were his carvings anyway. As long as they had those, there really was no problem.

The smell of the pie beckoned to him again and he gritted his teeth, deliberately turning away from it and walking out of the kitchen.

If I am not near enough to smell it, I will not be tempted by it. Right? Of course I'm right. So that's that.

He walked out of the room without so much as another sniff, closing the door behind him and walking over to pick up his carving tools.

If he couldn't ignore the pie, he would try to work. That nearly always distracted him.

Six

It was several hours later when Peter
walked in through Aden's front door,
heading straight for the kitchen, his arms
full of bags.

Aden had forgotten that it was shopping
day. But Peter didn't forget—he never
forgot. Even if Aden sometimes wished he
would. Peter was determined to help Aden,

even when his cousin wanted to left alone.

Goodness knows he had tried enough times to discourage Peter—without any success. It wasn't that he didn't appreciate his cousin's help, because he did. Peter was a great help to him. But he kept hoping that some day his cousin would stop pushing him to get out around his family and friends... to join the community again.

Aden kept working, having successfully forgotten for the moment about the pie sitting on his kitchen counter. It was only when Peter walked out of the kitchen a few minutes later with the dish in his hands, that Aden silently scolded himself.

He should have remembered about his cousin coming by today. He should have moved the pie... hidden it, or tossed it out. Peter would have questions and he would expect Aden have the answers to them.

Come to think of it, Peter had been the first person who started pushing Aden to start seeing other young woman in their community, to move on, to let go of Dawn.

Aden hadn't had the heart to tell Peter it was not that simple. Everyone in their circle of friends and family thought he was holding on to Dawn because he did not want to let her go.

He had no idea how to explain to them that he was holding on to her because he could not stand the idea of opening his heart again only to take a chance on losing the woman he loved... again.

The accident had been painful. The scars he wore were painful and difficult to live with, but the most agonizing part of the whole ordeal had been to lose the one person he had expected to share the rest of his life with.

She was gone and there was no getting back the time he had devoted to her, the part of his heart that had belonged to her, the plans they had made, the life they had shared... and had planned to share for the rest of their lives.

The idea of it all happening again was simply too painful to bear. He wanted no part of it. He was perfectly content to sit in his house, carve his wood, and watch everyone else grow old with the man or woman they loved dearly.

"So, who brought this? A girl?" Peter's voice was filled with intrigue and curiosity, just as Aden had known it would be.

"Yes." He answered simply, his voice nearly a growl as he tried to drop a hint to his nosy cousin.

"What girl? Is it someone I know?" Peter was obviously not taking the hint. In fact, Aden was certain there was even more excitement in his voice than there had been moments before.

Aden ignored his question and kept on working.

"*Kumme* now, Aden... which girl dropped this off for you? And what's the occasion? Girls aren't exactly known for dropping pies off for absolutely no reason."

Aden grunted again, but otherwise did not respond to his cousin's baiting.

"*Allrecht* then, I suppose you won't mind if I cut it and have a slice."

Aden turned, started to say something that would stop his cousin—and he knew, the moment he saw the expression on Peter's face, that he was caught. There must be something in his own expression that gave away what the pie actually meant to him.

When Peter held the pie up to him, he forced himself to shrug and then turn back to his work. Let Peter cut the pie. Let him eat a piece... or even two. Aden told himself he would not be tempted by it.

Moments later his cousin disappeared back into the kitchen. Aden looked over to the door every few seconds. He fully expected to see Peter walk back out with a plate full of pie, but his cousin never appeared and, after some time, curiosity got the better of him and he wandered into the kitchen.

"I knew it." Peter practically yelled from behind the kitchen door.

Aden jumped and dropped the chisel in his hand. It stuck in the floor at his feet, standing upright, the sharp end sunk into the linoleum floor.

"Peter, what are you doing? That was very nearly my foot." Aden worked to keep his voice calm, but his frustration had the words sounding harsh and cold.

Peter did not look the least bit sorry.

"There is a girl with a crush on you. Who is she?" Peter's voice was filled with curiosity and certainty.

"It is nothing like that at all." Aden was surprised at how tired and despondent he suddenly felt. He would likely never get Peter to believe him, but he knew the reason she had dropped off the pie had nothing to do with having a crush.

No one would ever... could ever... have a crush on him. And, even if she could... once she saw his scars in the light of day, she would for sure and for certain change her mind right quick.

The only evidence he needed to know the truth of his thoughts was the memory of his first trip into town after, well, after what happened to change his life.

After the accident, he had spent weeks in the hospital. The doctors had said his burns made him especially susceptible to infection and germs. Since it had been late fall, cold weather had begun to set in soon after the accident occurred.

Since illness often came with cold weather, the doctors had elected to keep him there, under observation—and mostly in isolation—so that he would not contract an illness, which would slow his healing.

Even after his release, the doctors had cautioned him against being around other people. They had insisted he isolate himself as much as possible in order to limit his exposure to germs.

Over a month after he was released from the hospital, he had finally been told by the doctors that it was relatively safe for him to be out in public.

Since he was the only one who could access his bank account, he knew that his only option for removing Dawn's name and to transfer the money he planned to give her family was to go and take care of it himself.

He had driven into town slowly, cringing with every bump the buggy wheels hit. He had chosen to park near the edge of town and walk some. The doctor had told him he needed exercise, and he figured less time in the buggy would mean less bumps.

That, as it had turned out, was his first mistake. Every single person he passed looked at him, and then looked away quickly. Several people had gasped loudly as they turned away. But the one reaction that had truly stuck with him all these years was the young girl who had actually screamed in fright at the sight of him.

He had been walking out of the bank, turning to walk to the craft store a few doors down with the intention of picking up some supplies for his carving. She had been walking along with her mother and had looked up at him with a smile on her sweet face.

Only seconds after looking at him, she had turned away and rushed around behind her mother, screaming as she hid behind her. Then she had moved as far away as possible as they walked past him.

Her mother had looked at him briefly, but said nothing until they had moved past him far enough that he could not have heard them anyway.

He had not stopped or looked back. He had walked into the store, collected his supplies with his head down, paid his bill and then walked as quickly as possible back to his buggy, his head still facing the ground and any hint of a smile gone from his face.

He had climbed back into the buggy and had somehow managed to make it back home before he'd collapsed.

He had not been back to town since.

After a few more weeks, the doctor had cleared him to return to Sunday service, and he had felt it was important to do so. But he did not attend the singings or the other community gatherings.

He told himself it was all for the best anyway. If he never took a chance to meet any of the other young women in the community, he would never be tempted to fall in love with one of them. And if he never fell in love, he could never be hurt again... the way he had when Dawn had been taken from him.

It had seemed like the perfect solution... until a wet schoolteacher had knocked on his door during a storm.

She had *kumme* into his house and his life—and she had ruined all of his plans.

Now she had him thinking of her. Again and again he would find himself thinking about her. Lying in bed at night... or soon after waking.

Sometimes, while he was eating, he'd find himself wondering what she was doing. He'd picture her face the way she looked when he had opened the door. The way she held out the pie, refusing to move, practically daring him to take it. When he didn't move, she had set it down at his feet and walked back to her buggy.

He remembered watching her as she left. He didn't like that she was disrupting his work, his sleep, and his appetite. He especially didn't like that it was getting harder and harder to push her out of his thoughts.

Even worse, he found himself wanting, wishing, hoping that she could be the one person who could look past his scars... even though he knew it was an impossible expectation.

What young woman, especially such a sweet and gentle one such as Beth, could possibly look past the hideous scars that were a permanent reminder of the accident that had forever changed his life?

He told himself it was ridiculous to hope for the impossible, but his mind and his heart were at odds.

* * *

Peter was there for another hour, putting things away, cleaning up a little, opening the curtains at nearly every window, and making a general nuisance of himself, but he did not ask about the pie or its maker again.

Aden eventually went back to work. And after awhile, Peter wandered into the living room to watch. He sat on the arm of the chair Aden typically sat in to read, while he quietly watched as Aden worked.

As much as Aden hated to admit it, his

work went much more quickly with the light streaming in through the front windows.

It felt as if hardly any time had passed before he stepped back and realized he was finished with the piece he had been working on for several weeks.

After a minute or two, Peter stood and moved over beside him, looking at the carving. He let out a long whistle. "It's amazing, Aden."

"*Danki.*"

"But you have to admit, cousin. It's much easier to carve when you have good light." There was a smug quality to Peter's voice that made Aden want to argue. But he didn't see a point, since Peter was right.

Peter stepped away, moving toward the front door, then stopped and turned back. "Want me to stay around and wait until it's ready to be delivered?"

Aden was already shaking his head. "*Nee.* The stain will need to be applied, and then it will need time to dry, at least overnight. Tomorrow is soon enough."

"*Allrecht.* I'll see you tomorrow then." Peter gave his cousin's shoulder a light punch and then headed for the front door.

Aden didn't turn around when he heard the door open—or after he heard it shut, or even when he heard Peter's footsteps on the porch stairs.

He just stood there... staring at the carving that somehow reminded him of a pretty schoolteacher.

Seven

At Sunday services that week, Beth found herself watching for Aden. She squirmed in her seat, then silently scolded herself for nearly falling off the bench when she spotted him at the back of the large barn.

He walked in and slipped onto a bench at the very back of the room, sitting quickly and ducking his head. It was obvious that he was doing everything possible to avoid drawing attention to himself.

She watched closely, trying to get a better look at him. The people in town who had told her about his accident all talked as if they knew he was scarred, but not one of them actually appeared to know the extent of scarring—or what parts of his body had been affected. Some of them had mentioned that they were pretty sure his face had been scarred, but again, no one seemed to be entirely certain.

That felt very strange to her, and she couldn't help but think that they must be trying to be vague on purpose. People must have seen him since the accident. How could they not know the extent of his scars?

Of course... if that is how he always lights his home, what visitor could possibly see anything clearly? The memory of how difficult a time she'd had navigating his dark rooms told her she might be mistaken about how easy it would be for someone to see Aden clearly. And his posture as he sat on the bench in the back of the room, up against the back wall, hunched in on himself so tightly told her he must take great pains to let anyone too close, even at Sunday services.

She watched him while everyone around him took their seats, foolishly hoping that he would look up and search her out in the crowd as well. But he never did. Instead, he looked down at the floor the entire time.

When the service started, she turned back toward the front and tried to focus her attention where it belonged, but in the back of her mind she continued to think about him. She just couldn't seem to stop.

When the last hymn had been sung, the last verse had been quoted, and the last words of weekly wisdom had been passed on, she stood with everyone else. When she turned to look at the bench where he had been seated, he was nowhere to be seen.

She made her way to the back of the barn, but she couldn't find him anywhere in the crowd. He wasn't inside. He wasn't outside. He was nowhere to be found.

She felt like she should have been surprised, but she wasn't, because it made sense that he would disappear quickly after Sunday services.

It was actually a testament to his faith that he even came. According to the people in town, he never came into any of the shops. A few people said they had seen him once or twice after his accident, but that he had stopped coming into town shortly after.

Given the cave-like lighting in his house, and his determination to stay far away from everyone, she was not the least bit surprised by that, though she felt unimaginably sad when she thought about it.

She couldn't figure out if he was truly hiding his scars or if he was hiding from places he had been with his fiance... places they had shopped, eaten, and played together... though she suspected it was more the first, especially given his behavior in service this morning.

Either answer was sad, but somehow the first one felt as if it would be much easier to overcome. If it were just his scars, all she would have to do would be to show him that no one was repulsed by him.

It wouldn't be easy, but she was convinced it could be done.

While she tried to think about a way she could convince him to go into town with her, she walked toward the house where the ladies were starting to set out lunch for the men.

She got no more than ten feet before one of her scholars stopped her, and then tugged her in the direction of his parents. She spent the next half hour being pulled from one set of parents to the next, each scholar excited about introducing their new teacher to their family.

She made a point to compliment each student, pointing out special things that she had learned about each one of them in the last few weeks. They were a delightful bunch of children and she felt immeasurably blessed to be teaching them.

While she walked among the families, meeting more parents and children she would be teaching the next year, she had a moment to thank *Gotte* for the opportunity to teach in this small community. There truly was no other job she was better suited to.

She had time to explore. She had time to visit. She had time to read. She even had time to explore the local library. For such a small community, she'd been surprised to discover their library was quite impressive.

There was no place in the world Beth was more at home than in a library. Surrounded by books, she always felt at her very best. It was the reason she had turned one room in each house where they lived into a small personal library.

Her love of books and knowledge made teaching the most logical thing for her to devote her time to. *Gotte* had blessed them in that area as well. Every new community they moved to had been in need of a teacher, which made it simple for her to find work right away, plus get to know the families in the community. She was blessed to have a job that allowed her to share her love of knowledge with young minds.

She only wished they could find a community where they felt as if they truly belonged. It always seemed as if they might have found a place to fit in the beginning. But after a time, that feeling faded and they began to feel the itch to move on.

Since her *mamm* had passed away, Beth could remember at least ten different towns they had moved to—some for only a short amount of time, while others for much longer. And each one had a definite point of time when they felt compelled to move on.

Yet each time they moved, Beth hoped it would be the last time. She prayed that they would find a place where they belonged... a place where they felt truly at home.

But as simple as it sounded, as wonderful as it would be, it had not happened. Until now.

This town was different in one way—so far—and that gave her hope. In this little town, she had found someone who had sparked her interest in a way that no one else ever had.

The man. The strange, gruff man who kept to himself. She often found herself thinking of him.

He was as prickly as a cacti, yes. But there was something different about him. Something that intrigued her and she was determined to find out what it was.

Eight

During the following week, Beth found an excuse to stop by Aden's house nearly every day. She brought him freshly baked bread, another pie, a stack of books, and fresh flowers from their garden.

The books she brought him were accepted with a nod and a brief comment of thanks. Then he withdrew to work on whatever it was he had in the corner of his living room.

When she tried to get close enough to see it better, marveling that he managed to get any work done in such low light, he turned and recoiled so suddenly from her, she retreated quickly and did not venture toward the corner again.

When she showed up the next day, he shoved a pile of books at her. Taking them, she noticed that they were the books she had brought him previously. Before she could speak, he told her he owned all but one of the books, which he had kept. Then he had complimented her on her taste in literature.

She had not expected such a thing—to learn that he was as well read as she was. It was a surprise, to be sure. Most people thought her being so well read was more than a little odd. And here finally was someone else who measured up. It was oddly refreshing.

The next day she delivered the pie, which he thanked her for with an odd little smile and what she thought might be considered a laugh. This time, when he moved to the corner, she followed right along behind him, holding her ground when he turned in surprise.

It was the first time she gathered enough courage to ask why he spent so much time in the dark.

His answer was clipped and stiff, his voice low and more than a little cold. "My scars upset people. It's better if no one has to see them."

"Even you?" She spoke quietly, smiling a little when his head jerked up at her question.

"What is that supposed to mean?" He stepped toward her a little, but not out of the shadows or near enough she could reach out and touch him.

"If you are only concerned about no one else seeing your scars, you can easily achieve that with the thick curtains you have at each window. But you keep the light low in every room, so low that there's no chance of even you catching a glimpse of your scars." She shrugged a little and turned away then, confident she had made her point.

He said nothing for nearly a minute. And then, when he did speak, he seemed much closer to her. He must have moved when she did, or else he had learned to move without making a sound because she had no idea he had moved so close to her before he spoke.

"If you were to see my scars, you would quickly run away from here, horrified at what you had seen."

She turned and looked up at him. "I would not."

She felt certain she could see something of his scars, but not clearly enough to know if they truly were as frightening as he seemed to think they were.

For a few moments, it seemed as if time had stopped. Neither of them spoke—or moved. Then he spoke again.

"Prove it."

He stepped closer to her. She could see his face more clearly than she had so far, but the room was still quite dark, so much so that he remained in the shadows.

"I'm not going anywhere." She hoped she sounded as confident as she felt.

Not that it will matter to him.

She felt certain he would believe whatever he wanted to believe. But still she waited, wondering if he would come even nearer. Out of the shadows. Into the light.

He stood his ground for a few moments, watching her, but then retreated to his corner. Without saying another word, he went back to work. After waiting for what seemed a long time with nothing but silence, she quietly left.

The next day when he opened the door for her, she was more than a little surprised to find that there was a light on in the front room. None of the curtains were open, and the room was still nowhere near as bright as it should have been, but there was light. Enough light so that she could actually see his face.

It only took a moment to see that his scars were intense, for sure and for certain, but honestly, they were nowhere near as frightening as she had expected.

She stepped into the room, handed him the loaf of bread she'd brought and looked up at him. He kept his head down, his eyes seemed focused on the loaf of bread in his hand, but he didn't back away from her.

They stood there for a long time, with her looking up at him while he looked down at the bread... or perhaps the floor. She really couldn't tell what his eyes were focused on. Then he mumbled something and turning toward the kitchen, walked out of the room.

When he came back, he walked over to

the wood he'd clearly been working with before she arrived and picked up his tools—without saying a word.

She moved closer, making a point to stay close enough to him so he would know she could see him... and wasn't bothered in the least to stand there looking at him. Actually, she was more than a little excited that he was even allowing her to watch him work. After all, it had been his plan to shock her.

Well, I guess I surprised him.

Beth almost giggled to find that things had worked out so well, but she held back her laughter. She felt pretty certain he would take it the wrong way. Still, she couldn't help but feel relieved at how things had turned out so far.

* * *

Each day she worked her way a little closer, surprised when he didn't object.

Either he was ridiculously determined to prove his point or he was actually getting accustomed to her presence.

It was oddly flattering.

She was also thrilled to see how much more light he let into the rooms when she was there. At first it was turning the lamps up a bit higher. Then it was the natural light coming from a window he'd left uncovered.

As she watched him, she was amazed by his talent to create beauty from a block of wood.

If only others could see the wonderful person that he was—and not let his scars scare them away.

After several days, she gathered up her nerve to approach him. She spoke carefully, doing everything possible to raise the subject gently, eventually getting around to asking him if she could touch his scars.

She had felt somewhat discouraged to find that her determination not to run away screaming when she viewed his scars up close had not managed to prove anything to him about his not being hideous.

She had no idea what else to try. She only knew that somehow she had to find a way to prove to Aden that she was not repulsed by him.

At least, that was what she told herself anyway. Whenever she thought about it, the butterflies in her stomach told her there might be yet another reason she wanted to be so close to him—close enough to touch him.

She tried hard to ignore such nonsense. Of course her motives had nothing to do with wanting to be close to him. She simply felt she should try and help the poor man to see the truth of his situation.

She told herself it was her duty as a *gut* neighbor and a *gut* Christian to help him. For sure and for certain, that must be why she thought of him at other times when they were not together. Her mind must be using the time to think of ways she might be able to get through to this very stubborn man. Aden Bontrager was indeed the most stubborn man she had ever encountered.

Of course that is it.

What else could there be?

There could be no other reason for it. Aden was a man in mourning and she was a teacher. She was not one bit interested in anything beyond giving a helping hand to someone in need of help.

Ach. Well, that was what she told herself. And she was trying oh, so hard to believe it.

The next step, of course, would be to prove to him that no one would be as repulsed as he seemed to expect. It would not be an easy road, but it was one she was determined to travel. Perhaps her not being afraid to touch him would help.

Nine

reaching up toward Aden's scarred cheek. His muscles under where her other hand rested on his arm were stretched tight and nearly vibrating as he strained to keep himself from stopping her... or running away.

When she did touch the puckered and

irregular skin stretched tight across his cheekbone, she concentrated on keeping her touch even and steady as she moved her hand slowly forward.

His eyes fluttered closed as she slowly moved her fingers. When her fingers stopped moving, her hand resting gently against his cheek, he let out a ragged breath.

"See. It's not so bad having me touch you."

He surprised her by reaching up to place his hand over hers. Then, with his eyes still closed, he slowly moved his head so that her hand slid back across his cheek until the edge of her hand was against his lips.

Warmth spread from where his hand lay over hers and where his lips pressed against her palm, robbing the muscles in her legs of strength and her lungs of breath. Still, she struggled to stay calm. It had taken so long to convince him that she could handle touching his scars. She would not ruin it now with her own unexpected response to his touch.

He held her hand there for several seconds, his breath tickling against the hairs on her arm, before he slid her hand further and kissed her palm gently.

Then once again, he moved her hand and held it against his lips for several seconds, while her breath jumped and stuttered in her lungs. Even when he allowed her to slide her hand away from his lips, he kept his hand on hers, holding it gently as she lowered it.

When she looked up at him, he opened his eyes and was looking at her with an intense expression she wasn't certain she wanted to interpret.

"You're absolutely right. It wasn't bad at all." His words might have sounded sarcastic if not for the husky quality his voice had taken on, and the way his words lacked strength. He was nearly whispering, but still managed... somehow... to sound annoyed.

She laughed. She couldn't help it. The laughter just bubbled up within her. His voice was ragged with emotion or nerves—she couldn't tell which—but still he held onto her hand, taking it in both of his, the rough, uneven skin of his right palm up against hers.

She managed not to shiver, but she wanted to. There was a strange feeling rushing all through her at his touch. Something she had never experienced before. The warmth that had started in her hand was working it's way up her arms and into her chest, making her heart beat unevenly and much more quickly than she was used to.

Her breath shuddered a little as she let it out slowly, but she was determined to stay calm and not let him see just what his touch was doing to her. If he misinterpreted her reaction, it would only set them back.

"You know, this is the first time

someone other than a doctor or nurse has touched me since the accident." His voice still held a huskiness that must be from whatever he was feeling.

Perhaps my touch affects him the same way his does me.

To him, she only nodded, more than a little uncertain of how her voice might be affected by the emotions that were rushing through her at the moment.

He did not let go of her hand. Instead, he moved a little bit closer to her. "You're not repulsed by me, then?"

She shook her head, smiling a little as she made a hasty decision to be bold. "I have absolutely no desire to run away screaming."

When he only stared, his mouth open slightly in obvious surprise, she went on, still smiling. "You are nowhere near the beast you would like everyone in town to think you are, Aden Bontrager."

* * *

It had taken every ounce of self control Aden had to keep himself from stopping Beth when she reached up toward his face. Every instinct he had developed about his scars over the last three years were telling him it would be a disaster to let her actually touch his face, and the weird skin the fire and gravel had left behind.

But she'd asked... and she insisted that nothing about his injuries bothered her even a little bit. In fact, she had been asking about his scars for days.

Every morning, she rode by his house on her way to the school to teach her little scholars. Then, nearly every afternoon, she had stopped in to see him, to bring him books, or deliver some sweet treat, and pretty much make a general nuisance of herself.

He wanted to be annoyed at her. He wanted to be angry with himself for enjoying her company as much as he did. He wanted to tell her to stop coming. He wanted to forget he had ever met her.

But he didn't.

He couldn't.

He felt guilty for being attracted to her. He wanted to be annoyed that she appealed to him so much, but he couldn't seem to muster any annoyance when she was around, or even after she had left and he found himself thinking about her.

He tried and tried, but he couldn't figure out what it was about her that made him yearn to see her. Or what made him think about her after she'd left, and while he worked. And especially when he took the time to relax in the evening with a cup of hot tea and a book. But think about her he did. She was never far from his thoughts.

As a matter of fact, he had thought about her strange request ever since she had first mentioned it days ago. Out of habit he had recoiled almost violently when she had spoken of it... and he had turned around to find her standing only a few inches from him.

She had closed her eyes, stepped back and turned away from him. He'd felt as if he had let her down. He had actually been annoyed with himself until the end of her visit... and afterwards, as well.

The next day she had made the suggestion again. He had forced himself not to jump away or do anything that might put that look of disappointment back into her eyes, but he had not been able to bring himself to allow her to touch his scarred skin, eventually shaking his head and turning away from her.

Today, when she had asked, he had not been able to say no again. Her eyes had been so full of hope, shining out from their depths to spill over him in a way that made him almost think she might just be *allrecht* with it after all.

He had steeled himself for her reaction.

He was prepared, he told himself, for her to scream or run away. Or worse, to turn away in disgust and find some quick and convenient excuse to leave and never return.

But then she touched him, and whether or not she was repulsed by the feel of his skin had been the last thing on his mind. The feel of her delicate fingers gently resting against the over-sensitive skin of his cheek had sent heat and desire rushing through him.

Her calm determination had teased him so much that he had not been able to resist touching his own hand to hers, reveling in the feel of her soft, delicate skin.

Kissing her palm had been an impulse, more to see how she would handle such intimacy than to judge her reaction to the feel of his skin and the scars there. Or so he had tried to convince himself. But it didn't work.

Now he had an entirely new set of

problems to deal with. He held her hand between his, looking deeply into her deep, golden eyes. He wondered if she realized her lower lip was trembling slightly, her chest was rising and falling rapidly, or that the pulse in her wrist was fluttering faster than a hummingbird's wings.

There was nothing in her expression that told him she was thinking of those things, but there were obviously some very deep thoughts in her mind at the moment.

Her eyes, which had been shining with amusement at his reaction to her only moments ago, were now filled with nerves and something else he was not ready to try to identify.

When that trembling lower lip disappeared between her teeth, he could no longer deny what he wanted... needed. He leaned forward ever so slowly, giving her ample time to move away if she wished.

She inhaled sharply, but did not move away in any direction. When he continued to move closer, her eyes widened in what he hoped was realization of his intentions. She looked down a moment, and then back up, her eyes firmly fixed on his. A moment later, her teeth let go of her lower lip and she exhaled a puff of breath.

He stopped moving forward then, trying to give her one last chance to move away, but she didn't move or do anything to give him a sign that she wished him to stop. He closed the distance between them ever so slowly, then gently touched his lips to hers for a brief moment.

He was prepared to step back quickly, but her eyes fluttered closed and she let out a delightful little sigh as their kiss ended. He took it as a sign, leaning forward as far as their still clasped hands would allow.

When his lips touched hers again, his breath caught in his lungs, trapped there with the bounding emotions he still was not quite ready to explore.

How long they stood there like that, he

could not determine, but she never pulled away or stepped back, and after a time he tilted his head a little and moved just a bit closer.

The feel of her soft lips trembling lightly under the pressure of his was more than a shock. He could feel his desire growing and rushing throughout his entire body, and he forced himself to step back.

She stayed right where she had been, a small smile on the lips he had just thoroughly kissed, her eyes closed, the lashes laying delicately against her cheeks.

He rubbed a thumb over the tiny hand he still held in his and her eyes opened on a tiny gasp.

Then, before he could talk himself out of it, he let go of her hand and wrapped both arms around her, pulling her even closer as he touched his lips to hers yet again.

Her hands fluttered against him as he kissed her, finally settling against his chest as he held tightly to her, not allowing so much as a breath of wind between them.

It was some time before he forced himself to break away from her and loosen his hold. As much as he wanted to go on kissing her, he knew it would not be right, here in the house with only the two of them.

When they did break apart, he was not the only one whose breath was coming a little too quickly. Her breath was coming in short little pants and she leaned against him as if her legs were as weak as his own felt.

He still held tightly to her. He told himself it had more to do with helping them both to stay upright, but he knew deep down that he was simply not ready to let go of her. Not yet.

How long they stood there like that, with her hands splayed against his chest, his arms firmly around her, their breath coming quickly, their hearts pounding furiously... he could not tell.

Several times, he caught himself looking down at her, watching where she had caught her lower lip between her teeth again. Something about it made him want to kiss her again, but he knew it not would be a *gut* idea, at least not just yet.

Gradually, he loosened his hold on her. Then he stepped back. The distance was nearly painful, but necessary, he knew, to keep them accountable, to keep their behavior honorable. With a sigh, he stepped even further away.

She looked up at him with an expression somewhere between regret and excitement, speaking quietly after a moment. "I suppose I should go."

Not entirely trusting his voice, Aden nodded, then moved with her toward the door.

At the door, just as he opened it for her, she turned unexpectedly, looking up at him with her eyes wide and her lower lip caught between her teeth again.

He couldn't resist. He knew he should, but he seemed helpless to resist. He kissed her again, purposely keeping one hand on the door and laying the other on her arm gently, not entirely trusting that he would be able to let her go if he took hold of her again.

She stretched forward a little, leaning into the kiss, and him, as she raised up on her toes, a little hum in her throat as he moved his lips slowly over hers.

And this time she was the one who let go and stepped back. "I really should go. I guess."

He nodded again, adding after a moment, "Will I see you tomorrow?"

"*Jah,*" she answered with a smile. And then, before he could even think of kissing her again, she was out the door and moving across the porch, down the stairs, and across the yard to his small barn.

He watched as she swung herself up into the saddle already on her horse. Then, he returned her wave as she started to move down the driveway.

He watched her until she was entirely out of sight. Then he remained at the door and continued to watch for several minutes more, as she rode alongside the road... until the road turned and he could no longer see the horse or it's rider.

Ten

Beth stood in the doorway, holding the screen open with one hand, while she held out the other toward Aden She struggled to control her smile at his obvious hesitance. In the past few days he had changed his mind about their outing at least a dozen times.

Honestly, the man is worse than some of

my scholars.

The thought had *kumme* to her when he had first waffled, and each time he had gone one way or the other, the urge to smile or laugh had only increased.

When she had first offered up the suggestion that he should *kumme* into town with her, he had been quick to reply with a firm negative.

She had tried not to push, but had made a point to bring it up each time she saw him, pointing out how well they had already done with what he had been certain would be a disaster.

Each time she mentioned that first time that he had allowed her to touch his scarred cheek, he'd smiled and taken the opportunity to kiss her again—once in full view of his cousin Peter.

If he had continued to refuse to *kumme* with her into town, she had told herself she would simply enjoy the kiss that most always closely followed her suggestion.

However, he had finally agreed, and then he had promptly changed his mind... several times.

When she had arrived with her list and her bicycle on the day of their adventure, Peter had saddled Aden's horses, prepared his large buggy, and gotten everything ready to hook up, then smiled a bit too smugly in her direction before leaving.

Secretly, she wished he had stayed. It might have been a bit easier to get Aden moving with Peter there to lend his opinion to hers. But he had left too quickly after preparing the buggy, waving from the yard before climbing up onto his horse.

When she had asked if Aden was ready for their trip to town, the look of panic on his face had rivaled her youngest scholar's when one of the older children had suggested she climb to the top of the metal climbing structure on their playground.

It had been all Beth could do not to laugh out loud at his similarity to a six year old girl.

After that initial panic, he had changed his mind several more times, but she had thought they were ready. She had made her way to the door, held out a hand to him, and waited.

He refused to move an inch. He simply stood there, his face in shadow, his feet stubbornly planted, his arms firmly at his sides.

She refused to give up, making a point to stand outside, holding the door wide open to admit plenty of light, and holding her hand out to him, giving him the choice while still requiring him to take the initial steps.

Though she knew, if he didn't *kumme* soon, she would be forced to go out and remove the saddle from his horse and return home to get their small buggy.

She still had errands she had to do in town.

And then, just when she was nearly

ready to give up, he moved. His steps were slow and his expression told her he was still fighting with panic, but she stood firm.

When he finally reached he... when his face was in full sunlight... she nearly gasped in shock. Fortunately, she controlled the impulse, knowing he would never have kept moving if she gave him any reason to change his mind again.

Her reaction was completely unexpected. She had expected his scars to be more pronounced in the bright light, but they were hardly noticeable. In fact, his face was quite handsome in the light, the scars only causing his face to look more rugged than she would have thought possible.

Contrary to what she expected, he had a *wunderbaar* face, strong and well shaped. His eyes were nearly always filled with sadness, but there were times it faded— usually when he kissed her.

She tucked the information away in her

head for later, already trying to figure out some way to tell him about her discovery. If she could convince him to open his curtains, light his rooms better, get outside more often, it could only do him *gut*.

Of course, it would likely make her attraction for him that much stronger. Not something she would complain about. Not one bit.

Also, she would have to find some way to tell him without making much reference to his scars. She knew he would essentially stop listening to anything positive if she even mentioned the scars, so strong was his self loathing.

If only he could somehow see this for himself...

The thought made her want to put a mirror up in front of him, force him to look at his reflection, and hope for the best.

Her experience with her *dat's* stubbornness and that of her scholars told her it would be a very bad idea. He would need to be brought round slowly, easily, when he was ready for it, not when it would be sprung on him suddenly and forcefully.

So she kept the information to herself, even while she offered up a prayer to *Gotte* that He would send someone along their path while they were in town who would essentially tell Aden the same thing she had just discovered, knowing there was a *gut* chance he would take the news better from someone he'd known for a long time.

At least she hoped he would.

* * *

Their drive into town was mostly a quiet one. Fortunately, Peter had chosen to hitch up Aden's covered buggy. Beth had a feeling if he had not, Aden would have simply unhooked one and replaced it with the other before leaving his house.

As he drove along the quiet country

roads, Beth took every opportunity to look at Aden's face. Even the small amount of light coming in through the window of the buggy was more than usually came in through his heavily covered windows and with all of his lamps turned down low.

Whenever she had asked Aden about his scars, he had made a point to change the subject or simply ignore her. And she had tried to broach the subject with Peter on multiple occasions, only to have Aden interrupt or distract them. So, she'd learned nothing of whether the accident had changed more than his looks.

She wished there was some way she could have known him before the accident. She was always cautious not to suggest any such thing to Aden though, certain he would take the comment badly.

She had seen for herself the differences in his carving. One of the shops in town, along with several members of the community, had work Aden had completed both before and after the accident—and there was certainly a difference there.

His talent was so very staggering. She could not help but wonder if it had more to do with the time he put into every piece now, or if there was more to it.

"Do you think it is possible that your faith has become stronger since the accident, Aden?" She spoke quietly, bracing herself for his reaction.

She had seen firsthand just how unpredictable his moods could be when asked what appeared to be a perfectly innocent question.

He looked over at her for a moment, his expression impossible to read. Then he looked back toward the road before answering. "I like to think it is. Why do you ask?"

She shook her head a little before answering him. "Mostly I think it must be stronger because your work is so much more reflective of it. Your talent looks to me as if it flows directly from Heaven."

He opened his mouth to speak, but said nothing. A moment later, he closed it and shook his head. Then, for the longest time, he sat there quietly... and she did the same.

His face was unreadable again. Beth did not wish to make him angry or to hurt him in any way. Since there was no way to tell how he was feeling from his facial expression, she decided that waiting would be best.

By the time they turned onto the road that would lead them into town, there was enough tension radiating from Aden that she could feel it hanging in the air around them.

When she looked over, his knuckles were white from the strength with which he held the reins.

She wanted to reach out to him, to place a hand over his, to lean into him and tell him that everything was going to be *allrecht*. But, truly she had no idea if her words would be true or false, so she was hesitant to offer them.

Only a moment later, she gave in to her impulse when she realized he was leaning back as far as he possibly could, attempting to hide in what little shadow there was in the buggy as they drove through the town. She placed a hand over his and squeezed gently.

"It's going to be *allrecht,* Aden." She kept her voice low, but did her best to infuse her words with hope.

"*Nee.* It's not going to be *allrecht.* This was a bad idea, Beth. No one in town wants to see me. They will run away, sickened by the very sight of me. I cannot do this." He had been slowing the buggy to park, but with his words, he sped up again.

He continued through town, making several turns until they were headed back the way they had *kumme.* She wanted to tell him he was worried for nothing. She wanted to tell him he would have to take this step one day. She wanted to push. But she knew there was little chance he would be convinced by her.

She was too close to him. He would think she was seeing him differently than everyone else would. She would have to be patient with him, cautious in her approach.

And she would have to be steadfast, never giving up on him. He needed to make the decision on his own if he was ever to be comfortable with it. She knew that, but accepting it was another thing entirely.

Once they left the town behind them, she leaned over a little, twining her arm around his. "This is *gut,* too. I have you all to myself."

He said nothing, but she could see the corner of his mouth turn up in a smile... almost a smirk. In turn, she smiled and snuggled a bit closer, looking out the window as they left behind the outskirts of the town as well.

They rode for a long time in silence. The

countryside slipped by and Beth watched with appreciation, marveling at the beauty her new home held and finding herself hoping that this might be the one time they would stay.

With that thought, she turned her head slowly, studying the man who sat beside her. She had never felt a desire to stay anywhere else. Could he be one of the reasons she wanted to stay here?

What would he think about it if he were? Would he be annoyed? Would he be happy?

Would he be at all interested?

An unexpected amount of concern wove its way into her with that question. Did she even really want to ask that question? Did she want to know the answer?

Thinking back to all the time they had spent together over the last couple of weeks, it became obvious very quickly that she did not really want to know the answer. Not yet, anyway.

She needed more time to figure out how she felt about all of this. Things were moving entirely too quickly for comfort.

Eleven

When Aden pulled the buggy into his yard, he turned toward Beth, an apology ready on his lips, but the expression on her face concerned him far more than their ruined trip into town.

She was looking off into the distance. Her eyes were clouded over and the usually smooth skin over her nose was scrunched together. She'd been very quiet for a large part of the ride. What exactly was going on in that head of hers?

He parked just outside of the barn, thinking back over the time they had spent together so far today, trying to pinpoint what he had done to put such cares on her delicate shoulders.

"Beth, is everything *allrecht?*" He spoke very slowly, weighing his words carefully. Had he upset her with his inability to go into town, or was it something else?

He wanted to ask, but she turned her head, a smile erasing all but the clouds in her eyes, as she answered, her voice its usual cheerful, bright, and sweet.

"*Jah,* everything is just fine."

Then she was stepping down from the buggy, walking into his barn and returning a few minutes later, leading her horse, who was already hooked up to her own much smaller buggy.

At that, he scrambled out of his buggy,

walking around to her. "Are you going so soon? You're not going to stay and..."

He fumbled around, trying to think of an excuse she might stay for, finally landing on the weakest one he could think of. "Have some tea?"

She kept walking the horse, moving past his buggy, out into his gravel driveway. *"Nee.* I really do need to pick up a few things in town today." She kept moving. He walked along beside her.

They were nearly to the end of the driveway before she stepped up into her buggy. He followed, struggling to find some words that would convince her to stay, to wait, to give him time to apologize and figure out what he had done wrong, but no words came.

And then she was seated, settled, taking the reins in her hand. A moment later, she turned to him with one last smile. "I will see you later, *jah?"*

He could only nod, still unsure of what

he could say that would make her stay.

Then, he could only watch as she pulled out onto the road, turning toward town. He watched as she went down the road, until she was out of sight, and then for several minutes he tried to figure out what exactly had happened on their drive back to his house.

Finally, he turned to tend to his own horse, unhooking the buggy while still wondering whether he could have done anything differently than he had.

Then he wondered about when he would see her again. He hoped it would be soon. It wouldn't be soon enough for him.

She had stopped by nearly every day after school. Would she do so again? And the next day was a visiting Sunday. There would be no service. Where would she go? Would she *kumme* and visit him?

Should he go and visit her?

He had no answers. The thought of facing her *dat,* without knowing what he had done to upset her, terrified him. What would the man think of him... of whatever he had done to upset Beth?

How would he react if Aden just showed up at their house? Typically, the youth in the community kept their courting to themselves until they were ready to declare their intentions to the entire community, but he and Beth were not teenagers.

While he thought it over, he saw to his horse, taking a bit more extra time to clean and brush the one creature he never had to worry about upsetting.

All the horse asked of him was a bag of food, along with water, brushing, and a warm barn to sleep in.

* * *

Beth drove quickly away from Aden's house, then slowed as she approached town. She wondered at her own behavior, at her reaction to Aden's reluctance.

For sure and for certain, there were things she needed to do in town, but nothing that could not have waited. The real question was why Aden's inability to go into town was such a problem for her.

She wanted to think that it was something simple. A part of her believed that Aden was being silly... and she found it difficult to go along with his determination not to set foot in town or be around other people. She wanted to tell herself that it meant nothing to her whether or not he came to town or attended the singings or other community events.

But deep down, she was beginning to see that it did mean something to her. His behavior would affect her own life going forward, if they went on the way they had begun.

She might not fit into every community they had moved to, but she was not about to shut herself away like a pariah. And she could not be someone who lived with a man who did that very thing, either. There was no doubt in her mind that it was precisely what he had been doing all these years.

Aden had tried to convince her, likely as he had tried to convince himself, that he was sparing the townspeople and the other plain folks a horrible sight, but what he was doing was hiding.

She could see it plainly now. He was hiding from his pain, from his loss, and from his anger. He was hiding... and hoping he would not have to deal with any of it if he stayed in his little house and hid himself away from the world. He would never be happy if he remained in hiding. He needed to find the courage to face the future.

But how could she get him to see that for himself?

Twelve

Beth sat quietly in the chair her dat
had put in his workroom specially for her,
watching the movements of his hands as he
pieced together the delicate parts of a
clock's inner workings.

Those same hands had carried her to
bed more nights than she could remember,
turned the pages of her favorite books time

and again, held her close whenever sadness about the loss of Mamm dragged at her, brushed lovingly over their beloved horses, and been a source of strength and encouragement each time they started over in a new community.

She could not help but wonder at why it was only now, since meeting Aden, and seeing what astonishing works of art came from his nimble fingers and strong hands, that she had begun to pay more attention to hands all around her.

From the ladies of the community who sat together quilting on a Saturday afternoon... to the butcher or the baker in town... to the older ladies who sat in the rocking chairs in town knitting as people rushed by, their hands working out the complex patterns with no instruction or attention whatsoever.

"Am I really so much more interesting than your book?"

A small laugh escaped Beth's lips as she

was pulled from her thoughts by Dat's question.

"Jah, you are, Dat. Always."

Beth laughed again as he went back to his work, shaking his head a little as he did.

She watched him for nearly a minute before shifting her attention back to the book in her hands, still thinking about Aden's hands and the breathtaking art they were capable of shaping.

If only she could get him to see all of the beauty in his life...

*   *   *

When Peter arrived at Aden's house the next morning, he was surprised to find Aden working in the barn. He stood just inside the doors for several minutes, watching his cousin as he repaired a shutter that had kumme loose from the house some time ago.

Standing there watching the simple movements, Peter had to marvel at how the hands that created such astonishing works of art could also wield hammer and chisel so easily to repair an old shutter.

"Well, don't just stand there staring. Kumme hold this for me."

Aden spoke gruffly, but Peter was well used to it by now. He'd long ago figured out that his cousin's bark was far worse and he had no bite to speak of.

With a smile, Peter moved over next to where Aden stood, holding the pieces of the shutter together where his cousin was pointing. Aden said nothing, but went back to work.

They worked mostly in silence for a long time, the only sounds being Aden's occasional directions and the sounds from outside. Birds chirping, a dog barking in the distance, the occasional sound of hooves and wheels or a vehicle's engine out on the road.

When they had repaired the shutter Aden had been working on and the four stacked beside the workbench, Aden muttered a thank you to Peter and turned to put his tools away.

Peter, still marveling at the change in his cousin, went off to complete his normal routine of cleaning up the house, putting away anything he had brought with him, and collecting any completed pieces that needed delivering.

Aden did not follow, and when Peter walked into the house, the sight that greeted him was a shock, to say the least.

Not only was the room clean, the lamps were turned up brighter than he had ever seen them. He could see everything without squinting and getting ridiculously close to it.

He stood there for several minutes at least, just looking at a room that very closely resembled what he remembered from before Aden's accident. It was as if he had taken a step backwards in time... well, almost. The front windows were still covered by thick, heavy, dark curtains. But the rest of the room was completely changed. It was cheery again.

Warm. Inviting.

He wanted to ask Aden what had brought about the change, but in the same thought he realized it would like as not be a bad idea to say anything that might push his cousin back the other way.

And that was the last thing he wanted to do.

*　*　*

In the barn, Aden smiled to himself as he thought about his cousin's reaction to all of the changes this morning.

He laughed as he ran the plane over the bottom of the door from his guest bedroom. Peter had not even seemed to notice where Aden had smoothed out the rocks on the driveway.

The job had taken several hours, but Aden had to admit that the end result was well worth the time spent. When he had awoken, restless, and been unable to concentrate on his work, he had decided to tackle some of the little jobs he had noticed needed doing for some time.

For some reason, when he had pulled into the driveway last night, he'd noticed just how rough the gravel drive was.

When he had walked with Beth to the road... and then back after she'd left, he had found himself wondering why it had never bothered him until now. And then, when he'd walked back inside the house, he had taken a moment to look around him, seeing the rooms as if he were a guest.

What he had seen made him think, but even worse, had made him feel ashamed. He had been hiding away, yes. But he had failed to do the things that were his responsibility.

He had decided to change that.

The driveway had been first, though there was little he could do without more rocks to fill in the worst of the ruts. He had done what he could to smooth out the rocks where they had piled up, grateful that the ground underneath was soft enough to give a bit when he tamped down on the rocks.

Then, he had taken down the shutters which were obviously in need of attention or repair. He'd finished with the least difficult of them just as Peter had arrived and offered to lend a hand.

Aden would have liked to see Peter's face when he walked into the house, but he'd contented himself with his cousin's reaction when he had kumme into the barn and found Aden working.

He had only caught a glimpse of Peter's surprised face, but he knew he would never forget the expression on the young man's face.

For too long, Aden realized, he had been

a terrible influence for his young cousin, not to mention a dreadful burden. He had allowed his self pity to keep him from being the man Gotte wanted him to be.

That, too, will have to change.

*　*　*

It was hours later, when he and Peter were in the barn caring for the horses, when his cousin asked a question Aden had not allowed himself to even think about yet.

"So, how did your trip into town go?"

He fumbled and nearly dropped the hard bristled brush he'd been using to smooth Peanut's coat. And a moment later, when he didn't answer, Peter went on.

"I'm going to take that to mean it did not go well."

Aden only nodded.

"What happened?"

Peter's blunt question had Aden searching for answers. It would not take long for the truth to find its way to his cousin... and every other youth in town. But did he have to tell the young man everything or could he possibly just admit to losing his nerve and leave it at that? Perhaps that would be enough for now.

"Aden..." The hand on his shoulder startled Aden, and he did drop the brush then.

Quickly he bent to retrieve it, but Peter was quicker.

"Did you even make it into town?"

Aden shook his head, shame washing over him again at his failure and the disappointment in his young cousin's voice.

"So, is Beth allrecht with it then, or is all of this some sort of busy work to take your mind off what happened?"

Peter's lightning quick understanding of the situation surprised Aden. How could this young man who had only just begun his rumschpringe... who had only begun to spend time with the youth of the community in a courting capacity... how could he be so much wiser than his years?

He took a moment, but answered as honestly as possible, certain now that his cousin would see through anything other than the absolute truth.

"It's a little of both, actually. Beth did not take my hesitance well." When Peter only nodded, he went on. "As for all of this, I do not know why it took me so long to see it, but I finally realized how much I have been letting go, and I decided to do something about it."

A moment later, he added, "Any distraction is purely a side benefit," to which, Peter laughed.

*   *   *

When Peter headed for home, Aden tried for a long time to work, but no matter how hard he tried to concentrate, he could not.

After nearly an hour of just standing in

front of the slab of wood, he admitted to himself that he was not going to get anything done. And it was obvious that Beth was not going to come by.

If she will not kumme to me, I will have to go to her. He was suddenly thankful he had driven her home that first night they had met. If he had not, he would have no idea where she lived and who knew how long it would take to find someone who knew. Someone who would be willing to tell him.

Once the decision was made, it was no time at all before Aden was seated on his horse and heading down the drive, toward the road.

All the way from home Aden had thought about what he wanted to say to Beth—or her father, when... if... they opened the door for him. Since he had no idea who it would actually be at the door, he had been trying to think over what he could say to each of them.

He could not imagine that her dat would be all that welcoming to the young man who had hurt his precious dochder.

And Beth is obviously still upset with me. Otherwise, she would have stopped by on her way home from school.

The closer he got to her house, the better he felt about his plan to go to her. Even with the disaster of the day before, his appearing at her house, in bright daylight, on his horse for all to see would show her he was willing to try and get past his issues with allowing other people to see him and his scars.

The one thing he did not count on was the sight that greeted him when he reached the driveway to their house.

He sat, slumped now a little in his saddle, watching as Beth embraced a man who was certainly not her dat.The joy on her face was evident, even from so far away.

She had both arms around him, and he

had tucked her under one arm, and was walking back to where her dat stood, on the porch waiting for them. While Aden watched, Beth walked with the man to where her dat stood. Then he embraced the man, too.

He knew that Beth and her dat had lived in several different communities. More than one person in town talked about how all the young men looked at her.

Perhaps this man was someone she had left behind. Maybe he had kumme to take her back with him.

Aden rubbed a hand over his chest where a sudden, sharp pain exploded. He gritted his teeth against the pain, turning the horse away at the same time, heading back the way he had kumme. He had no reason to sit there and watch as Beth embraced another man.

A man who is not disfigured... a man who can give her the life she deserves... a man who she would never have to worry over being seen in public with.

He wanted to believe that she would not be so superficial, especially given her previous behavior, most especially given how she had tried to convince him that the scars did not bother her.

But her own behavior seemed to prove that she was, indeed, more interested in superficial beauty.

Thirteen

Aden heard a knock. Foolishly hopeful that it could be Beth at the door, he went to answer and was surprised to find the bishop on his front porch.

"Bishop Beiler, it is *gut* to see you." He stepped back, opened the door to admit his *freind*.

"Aden, how have you been?"

"I have been *gut*... very *gut*, Bishop. And you?"

"*Jah,* I have been *gut* as well."

They stood a moment before Aden moved toward the small grouping of chairs behind them. "Tea?"

The bishop nodded and Aden went to the kitchen to get the tea. While there, he tried to decide if he should ask his *freind* about the situation with Beth. Would he even know her well enough to answer?

Would she feel as if Aden were perhaps speaking out of turn about her?

Fortunately, the decision was sort of made for him when he returned to the living room with the tea. They chatted about the weather, Aden's health, the bishop's family.

Aden had just figured out how to talk about it in a way that would hopefully answer his concerns and not betray Beth at the same time, when the bishop asked him how things had been going for him lately.

"It is funny that you ask." When the bishop only made a little "hmm" sound, Aden went on.

"Just yesterday, I made the decision to go into town." He stopped a moment to give his *freind* time to comment, but he said nothing.

"It did not go so well."

The bishop only nodded.

"I managed to get all the way to town, and then, when it came time to park the buggy, I could not do it. I turned right around and drove back here."

Another "hmm" was the only answer he got.

"Am I being ridiculous? I mean, it's been years. I should probably find a way to move on, *jah?*"

There was no "hmm" this time, only a thoughtful nod and silence.

"I am being ridiculous then?"

It was several long seconds before he

answered. "Aden, have you ever stopped to think that this determination of yours to keep yourself hidden away is a form of pride?"

Aden sat back in shock. Pride? How could his wanting to protect people from having to look upon his frightening features prideful?

"I am sorry, Bishop. I do not understand at all how it could be pride." He shook his head at the very idea and waited for the bishop to explain.

The bishop was already nodding. "What I am saying is that you have convinced yourself you are hiding yourself away to protect everyone else."

Aden was nodding, even as the bishop went on. "However, I believe it to be more about your worries over how people see you."

When Aden started to speak, the bishop held up a hand to stop him. "I know. You're going to say that is what you are doing, but you're doing it to protect others."

Aden was already nodding again. *"Jah.* That is it exactly."

Bishop Beiler shook his head then. "But it is not so simple, Aden. You are hiding away to protect yourself from what others think of you. You can tell yourself all you want that it has more to do with protecting them, but I do not believe that is the case."

Aden started to shake his head, protest again, but the bishop went on.

"When is the last time that you truly looked at your scars... at your face in a mirror... or your hands, with anything other than loathing?"

Aden opened his mouth to speak, but found that he had no idea how to answer the question.

"I thought as much." was the bishop's answer. "You have convinced yourself that you are hideously frightening, and that the people of our community must be protected."

Aden was nodding before the bishop stopped speaking, adding in his agreement as soon as he could.

"*Jah,* that is just what I was thinking of." He shuddered, thinking of the young girl who had hidden behind her mother, clearly terrified of him... of his face.

"But don't you see? You are remembering one incident, something that happened when you were barely healed, perhaps before you should have even been out and about, while the accident and all that went with it was still fresh."

Aden regretted, for the first time, telling the bishop about the little girl and her mother, but before he could say anything, the bishop went on.

"You are allowing that one event to forever alter the course of your life, worrying over something that happened so long ago, and has no real bearing on who you are now or what you look like."

Aden started to object again, but

stopped mid-thought, instead focusing on something else the bishop had said. "What I look like... what exactly does that mean?"

"It means that there is nothing frightening about your appearance, Aden. You have healed much since the accident." He laid a hand on Aden's shoulder before going on. "Your scars will forever be a part of you, *jah*. But you have an idea in your head about how you look, and I believe it is not at all truthful."

When Aden said nothing, the bishop went on. "When was the last time you looked at yourself in the mirror?"

Aden stopped to think about that—and it took no time at all to discover that he had no answer. He could not actually remember the last time he had really looked at himself in the mirror. When he shaved, he only used a half mirror.

Because of his scars, he had been given special permission to use an electric razor, which was much quicker than the traditional way, so he had very little time to actually look at his face, only to see that all of the hair had been removed.

He thought then about Beth's reaction to his face, to the scars on his cheeks and hands.

She had not been one bit afraid of him. She had not been repulsed or disgusted.

Quite the opposite, in fact. And she had said more than once that he was not the beast he thought himself to be.

Could it be true? Had he spent so much time focusing on what he had once looked like, that he was not giving himself a chance to see the truth?

Without giving himself time to argue or reconsider, he got up and went to the bathroom, taking the lamp next to him along so that he would not have to light the one in that room only to blow it out a moment later.

When he stepped into the bathroom, he moved to the mirror right away, not taking any chance of losing his nerve. He braced himself for a horrific sight.

What he saw in the mirror both shocked and surprised him. His face looked nothing like it had the first time he had looked in this same mirror, just after he'd left the hospital and kumme home.

Jah, the scars were still there, but there was nothing frightening or disgusting about them. In fact, they had faded and smoothed out in a lot of places.

No, he was not what many women might consider handsome, but considering what he had been through, how long he had spent in the hospital, all of the damage that had been done by the accident itself and then the fire afterwards, it was nearly a miracle his face looked as normal as it did.

He owed Beth an apology. The bishop was absolutely right. He had been holding on to a very frightening image, and he needed to let it go and move on.

He thought again of the young man he

had seen Beth embracing just that afternoon. Was there still time to convince Beth to give him a chance? Another chance? Or would he be too late?

He would have to hurry.

* * *

Aden nearly lost his nerve again when the man he had seen hugging Beth answered the door. He stood there, with no idea what to say to a man that could very well be his competition for Beth's heart.

Before either of them could say a word, Beth walked into the room. With a puzzled look on her face, she walked to the door, stopping just behind the man.

"Hello, Aden. What a nice surprise."

It gave Aden the courage he needed to speak up.

"If you have a minute, Beth... could I speak to you, please?" He gestured widely, hoping she would take the hint and *kumme* outside to speak with him.

She nodded and stepped around the man in the doorway, turning as he moved as if to follow her. "Joshua, could you please tell *Dat* I will be back soon?"

He nodded. "Are you sure you don't want me to *kumme* with you, Bethie?"

"There's no need. I'll be back soon." She smiled as she answered. Aden could practically feel the warmth coming from her... but it was for the man in the doorway, not for him.

When she turned, the smile had faded a bit, but she started to walk down the steps and he followed quickly, determined to do or say whatever he needed to convince her to give him another chance.

"Beth," he began, but she held up a hand to interrupt him.

"I really don't have a lot of time, Aden. Joshua has *kumme* a long way, and he is leaving again tomorrow morning."

Her words threw him off. Together with

her complete lack of a smile, it felt as if his chance to convince her of anything was slipping away.

"I won't keep you long. I only wanted to apologize for my behavior when we drove to town."

"It's fine, Aden. I know it couldn't have been easy for you." There was a tone to her voice that made him think she might simply be trying to get rid of him at this point.

Feeling certain his chance had already passed him by, he resolved to speak his mind, to just put everything out there for her to know. What could it hurt now?

"So, this is it, is it? You've made up your mind, then? There's no chance for us? Is it to do with town at all, or is it the scars, after all? I suppose you'll be going with him tomorrow, then, when he leaves."

He gestured toward the house, turning away from her and taking several steps toward the barn before she answered.

"As a matter of fact, I will, but not for

the reasons I'm sure you think."

He turned back then. "What other reasons could there possibly be, Beth?"

She laughed then. "Perhaps because his wife, my sister-in-law, asked for me." And before Aden could say a word, she stepped forward, pushing a finger into his chest when she got close enough. "Not that you've given me a reason to stay here, Aden Bontrager... or a reason to *kumme* back."

It was several seconds before she added, "But I have to *kumme* back for my scholars. They enjoy having me as their teacher and I would not just leave them.

"So, you'll be back then?" He asked as he took hold of the hand pressing into his chest and pulled her close, wrapping both arms around her as she playfully struggled against him.

"*Jah,* I'll be back next week." She ducked her head, likely to hide her smile, but he could feel the warmth of it already. He tightened his hold a bit before speaking again, his voice soft and low.

"And when you *kumme* back, you would be willing to give me another chance?"

"Perhaps." She answered so quietly he could barely hear her, but the unmistakable sound of hope in her voice had his own smile widening.

"*Gut.* Then I have plenty of time to work on my issues with going into town."

She looked up then and he went on.

"I will go into town every day while you are gone. I will go into each and every shop and speak to as many people as I possibly can. They will all be sick of me by the time you get back, but we can still go into town as much as you want, and as often as you want. I will set up a shop in town if you like. I will do whatever I need to do to show you I am a changed man."

With the last words, he kissed her, not caring one bit if the man in her doorway, who he now assumed to be her brother, could see them or not.

It was nearly a minute later when they broke apart, when she answered him. "That sounds absolutely perfect. I can hardly wait."

Epilogue

Beth stood in front of the small, plain tombstone. Her hand was tucked tightly into Aden's even as his other hand squeezed her shoulder gently.

Only a few minutes after they'd arrived, he had wrapped his arm around her and pulled her close.

She knew it was his way of

communicating his contentment, and she was grateful for it, but it also helped keep her from being chilled by the crisp fall breeze currently blowing autumn leaves all around.

As she stood quietly waiting, head bowed in respect, she sent up her own silent prayer of thanks.

If anyone had told her a year ago that she would be about to say her vows to a man she had met only weeks after moving into town... a man who had done everything he could initially to push her away and scare her off, she would have thought they were telling a ridiculous joke.

The story of their courtship would be one worthy of the books they both enjoyed so much. Not only had her determination helped to tame her beloved beast, she had finally found a community to call home.

Their neighbors had welcomed her and *dat* and made them feel as if they finally belonged.

It was almost like her own little fairy tale come true.

Turn the page

for exclusive

Bonus content

DISCUSSION QUESTIONS

1) Peter went by Aden's house every day. He helped around the house, ran errands, brought supplies, and made deliveries. Do you think Peter enjoyed spending time and helping his cousin or did he do it just because he was asked?

2) Do you think Peter went above and beyond when helping his cousin? Did this have more to do with his plain faith, or was it just his way of living out Christ's command, *"Do until others..."*?

3) Because Aden was horribly disfigured, Peter was the only person he had contact with day to day... what would you do if you were too embarrassed or traumatized to be around other people? Who would you trust enough to allow them to see you, when you shut the world out?

4) Before the accident, Aden worked full-time at a company where he built cabinets. His carving was something he did for fun... and to make extra money. After the accident, carving becomes Aden's only source of income. Peter delivers Aden's beautiful carved pieces of artwork to the shops in town or directly to the person who ordered the item. How do you think Aden's recovery and isolation would have changed if he had been unable to survive solely on his income from carving?

5) Is it possible that Peter's continued determination to help his cousin in some way enabled Aden to keep himself locked away? What might have happened if Peter had stopped helping his cousin?

6) Aden and Beth would never have met if it had not been for a sudden

thunderstorm and an unexpected bicycle accident. I personally believe that God has an all-encompassing plan for each one of us, and He sometimes allows things to happen in an attempt to keep us on that path, or else nudge us back onto it. Do you believe this was God's way of putting Beth and Aden together?

7) Do you believe that Beth's determination to push her way into Aden's life had more to do with her attraction for him, or because she felt sorry for him, or was it possibly God's plan all along — and she was simply responding to God's prompting by way of the Holy Spirit?

8) Do you believe that God putting Aden and Beth together had more to do with Beth helping Aden to move past his traumatic accident? Or the love they found in each other... or both?

9) Beth shares several similarities to Belle from the original story. She loves to read. She endeavors to share knowledge with those around her. She feels a bit out of sync with the world around her. The plain community Beth and her father moved to are not as old-fashioned as some Amish communities, but they are also not as progressive as some. They are somewhere in-between. The community's acceptance of her has much to do with this. Do you feel that Beth would be just as easily accepted by our modern world if she were not Amish?

10) Many people in our world tell us we should be true to ourselves, but inevitably, those who are different from the "in crowd" are treated harshly or ridiculed by their peers. What can you do to help change this? How can you help yourself and others around you learn to be happy... without changing to please others?

ABOUT THE AUTHORS

Naomi Miller mixes up a batch of intrigue, sprinkled with Amish, Mennonite, and English characters, adding a pinch of mystery, and a dash of romance!

Naomi's days are spent focusing on her writing, editing and homeschooling her grandchildren. She loves her career as an author, blogger and inspirational speaker.

She schedules several book events each year and enjoys the opportunity to meet readers face-to-face. When she's not rushing to meet a deadline, Naomi loves to make time to attend writing conferences, workshops, and other author events.

Whenever time permits, Naomi can be found in one of two favorite places. . . the beach and the mountains. . . usually with a book in her hand.

Naomi loves traveling with her family, singing inspirational/gospel music, taking daily walks, and witnessing to others of the amazing grace of Jesus Christ.

Ruth Miller writes sweet Amish romances filled with faith, fun and forgiveness. Her interest in the Amish began with her name. She went in search of plain roots and was dismayed to discover there were none. Still, she travels to Amish country at least once each year for research and fellowship purposes. *And for fun as well.*

Ruth holds the plain people in the highest regard and believes they provide us with an example of the sort of Christ followers we should all aspire to be. In the high tech world we live in, we may not all be able to *"go Amish"*, but that is no reason we cannot incorporate some of their principles into our everyday life. Simplicity, living with less. Appreciating nature, forgiving others more readily, and trusting in God are values that can only make our lives better.

When Ruth isn't writing, swimming or reading, she is bragging to her friends about her precious babies. Family comes first with Ruth and she cannot get enough time with hers.

ABOUT THE PUBLISHER

Christian Publishing for HIS GLORY

S&G Publishing offers books with messages that honor Jesus Christ to the world! S&G works with Christian authors to bring you the best in "inspirational" fiction and non-fiction.

S&G is proud to publish a variety of Christian fiction genres:

inspirational romance

young reader

young adult

speculative

historical

suspense

Check out our website at

sgpublish.com

BOOKS BY NAOMI

Blueberry Cupcake Mystery
Christmas Cookie Mystery
Lemon Tart Mystery
Pumpkin Pie Mystery
Chocolate Truffle Mystery
Peach Cobbler Mystery

A Mother for Leah
A Suitor for Rebekah

Sophie Finds a Family
Sophie Celebrates Thanksgiving
Sophie's New Home